The Jane Goodall of Goats

a novel about the mammal brain

Loretta Graziano Breuning, PhD

Inner Mammal Institute

Inner Mammal Institute
InnerMammalInstitute.org
Loretta@InnerMammalInstitute.org

Books by Loretta G. Breuning, PhD

- **Habits of a Happy Brain**
  Retrain your brain to boost your serotonin, dopamine, oxytocin and endorphin levels

- **The Science of Positivity**
  Stop Negative Thought Patterns By Changing Your Brain Chemistry

- **Status Games**
  Why We Play and How to Stop

- **Tame Your Anxiety**
  Rewiring Your Brain for Happiness

- **I, Mammal**
  How to Make Peace with the Animal Urge for Social Power

- **How I Escaped Political Correctness**
  And You Can Too

- **14 Days to Sustainable Happiness**
  A Workbook for Every Brain

- **Why You're Unhappy: Biology vs Politics**

Dedicated to the many
readers who share
my view of reality.
Thank you! What a gift!

1

Welcome Home

I inherited a goat farm from my uncle five years ago. When his will was read, I was not thrilled by the news because I was busy enough without having goats to manage. I should add that it was a money-losing farm – my uncle's retirement hobby.

But it was near our home, at the other end of our small California town, so we got in the car to check it out. The kids fell in love with the goats and begged my husband and me to keep it. Frank thought it would give them a good grounding in reality, and my ears perked up when they pledged to do chores. So we looked for a way to make it work.

We calculated that we could fund the place out of savings for eighteen months if we sold our house and moved into the farmhouse. Then it would have to generate income. But how?

Frank suggested creating a goat cheese. I say "create" because he's a marketing consultant and always dreamed of launching his own product. I was a marketing professor, so I could relate.

Before making the final decision, we sat down with the couple who ran the farm for my uncle. Bunnie and Buck lived in a cottage behind the farmhouse and worked from a trailer next to the goatyard. We stopped snickering at their barnyard names as soon as we saw how skilled they were. They managed the infrastructure and the finances as well as the animals. "You won't need to get involved unless you want to," Buck said. They walked us through the books and we were impressed at how organized they were.

Bunnie and Buck had raised their children on the farm and assured us that they wanted to stay. They'd welcome us as neighbors, they said, and even offered to oversee repair work on the farmhouse before we moved in. So we put our house on the market and planned to move in the next month.

When we arrived on moving day, the kids jumped out of the car and ran to the goats. I was surprised to hear fifteen-year-old Matt talk to them in an animated tone. Twelve-year-old Andrea stared at the goats as if to decode their every move. I put my chores aside to enjoy the moment.

Suddenly, a goat fight erupted. One goat reared up on its hind legs and lunged at another.

"Stop! Help!" Andrea shouted as she ran to get Buck or Bunnie. "They're getting hurt!"

Matt shouted after her, "It's okay, they stopped." But a minute later, a goat crashed its skull into another goat's skull with its full body weight. Both kids shouted at once. "Help!" "Buck!" "They're gonna kill each other!"

"They'll be fine," Buck said running over. "It's normal goat behavior. They have thick skulls for just this reason."

"But it must hurt," Andrea said. "Can't you do something?"

"If I separated them, they'd start over as soon as they got back together. They fight until they clarify the dominance hierarchy. Don't worry. It doesn't last long. It's nature."

"Oh yeah, we saw that in a nature video," Matt said. "With monkeys and wolves and horses."

'I remember that. They fought until one gave up." said Andrea. "It made me sad."

"You may see it different soon," Buck said. "Come out and watch whenever you want. You'll see that they're very motivated by food. If a weaker individual gets between them and the food, they shove it. Like a toddler grabbing a toy from another toddler. We're all born with this impulse so it takes work to restrain it."

"Do the goats get hurt?" Andrea asked.

"They learn to protect themselves by getting out of the way of stronger individuals. They only fight when both goats think they're stronger."

The kids started shooting video of the goats and Buck went back to his chores. I thanked him for teaching the kids, but I was worried about my own chores. "Kids, we have a mountain of boxes to unpack to be ready for school on Monday."

"Moooom," they both bleated.

The kids didn't know the real source of my time pressure. Frank was in a hurry to start up our cheese business, so I promised to work on it in the morning. Frank called it the "branding meeting" and was greatly looking forward to it.

2

Cheese Biz

Saturday morning, I was making tea for the meeting when Bunnie appeared at our back door with homemade blueberry muffins. I was glad for the distraction because I had mixed feelings about the cheese business. It seemed to me that the world had a lot of cheese already. I didn't see how a new cheese could make money.

We thanked Bunnie for the delicious muffins and then got down to business. The kids hovered over us, so I assumed they wanted more muffins. But I noticed that they were listening with interest. I was glad for them to get real about money, so I looked at Frank and he invited them to sit down.

He explained that we had eighteen months of runway. He didn't say it in a panicky way, but he wanted them to understand that we'd have to sell the farm if the cheese didn't take off.

"Let's start by naming our cheese," Frank said.

"Stinky cheese!" Andrea said.

"That's dumb," Matt barked.

Frank explained the concept of brainstorming. "We take turns making suggestions, and no criticism is allowed on the first round. We'll judge the suggestions after we generate a good list."

I suggested "Chèvre" and Frank said "that's confusing and unpronounceable."

Matt suggested "Pasty Cheese" since goat cheese looks like paste to him. Frank said, "The name should have culinary appeal."

"What happened to not criticizing?" I said.

Then the doorbell rang.

Our next-door neighbor Suzi introduced herself. "I noticed you moving in yesterday. Usually I just see that older couple and hear all those goats."

"Our farm is fully permitted," I said, feeling strangely defensive. We introduced ourselves and offered Suzi a muffin.

She sat down and took a bite, and then said, "I came to tell you that your goats need more love. I'm an empath, so I know these things. When I see them fight, I know they're not getting enough compassion."

"That's not what it means," Matt said.

I put my arm around him and said, "They get the best of care from our manager Buck. I'll introduce you to him if you'd like."

"I wanted to tell *you*. Anyways, I have to leave for work now. I'm a sobriety coach and I work nights and weekends."

The door shut behind her and we all exhaled.

"Why did you involve Buck?" Frank said.

"Why didn't you let me explain the facts to her?" Matt said.

"What's a sobriety coach?" Andrea said.

"I'm proud of you for trying, Matt, but I didn't think she'd listen. She obviously just wanted to flaunt her empathy. It's the modern equivalent of having bigger horns."

"Will you tell me what's a sobriety coach after the brainstorming?" Andrea said. I was glad she was paying attention.

"I have a suggestion," Frank said. "Everyone think of good names this week and bring them to next Saturday's meeting. For now, why don't we go to the goatyard and learn more about what Buck does."

While we walked there, I explained that "a sobriety coach helps people learn to resist the temptation to make bad choices."

"Like grabbing another kid's toy?" Andrea asked.

"She means drugs and alcohol," Matt said.

"Anything that feels good now but hurts you later," I said.

We stared at the goats for a long time, mesmerized by the sight of them flowing between the milking area, the feeding area, the sleeping area, and the open space. Buck had it perfectly choreographed and told us how he made it happen.

Ch 3
Browsing

Early Sunday morning, the doorbell rang. It was Suzi.

"I can't sleep because I keep feeling the suffering of your goats. I will need to talk to Buck."

"I think he's still sleeping and I hate to bother him on a Sunday."

"No, he's awake. I heard him call the goats. I'll just go around back."

She ran down the front stairs and around the side of the house. I shouted "Suuuuziiii." I didn't expect her to stop – I just wanted to alert the family. We all ran out the back door to catch up with her.

There, we were stunned to see Buck sitting calmly with her at the picnic table, while Bunnie put a glass of juice in her hand. We stopped at a distance to listen.

"The welfare of your goats has kept me up all night. I tried to manifest dreams of them in a green meadow, but all I see is that brown grass you have. How can you be so uncaring!"

"That's not what goats eat," Buck said. "They don't eat off the ground because soiled plants cause intestinal worms. They instinctively eat from plants that are elevated, which is called browsing as opposed to grazing. So that grass has nothing to do with their diet. We have a veterinarian monitoring their diet, by the way."

I was grateful to Buck for handling this, but it didn't seem fair to leave it all to him. So I walked closer and said, "You didn't sleep last night because you were working the night shift."

"You're not hearing me," Suzi said with her eyeballs practically popping out.

"I hear you but I don't agree with you."

"You're really insensitive," she said, and turned to leave. She did this slowly to give me time to run after her, but I didn't.

I thanked Buck and Bunnie profusely and hoped this wouldn't get under their skin. I hoped the same for myself, since we had a big day of unpacking ahead of us.

Bunnie said "Can I have a minute with you for an immediate issue?" I smiled, and she continued. "Your uncle used to welcome visits from local schools. He understood the liability, but he loved the kids. We'll continue that?"

"Hmm. Let me discuss it with Frank."

"Well...the calendar shows a visit for tomorrow morning. Maybe I should have told you sooner."

Hmmmm. Community relations. Might show us a better side of the community than we saw today. "Fine. Actually, I'll come and watch since I only go to campus on

Tuesdays and Thursdays." I should assess the liability for myself, I thought. Bunnie looked so happy that I suspected the school program came from her as much as my uncle.

When I got back in the house, Andrea asked, "Why is Suzi mad at us?"

"Why is she a jerk?" Matt said.

"How did you know she worked the night shift?" Frank said.

"I don't know I don't know I don't know." I couldn't come up with good answers because I was rattled by the thought of having such a manipulative and intrusive neighbor. But it's wrong to vent in front of your kids, so I bit my tongue very hard.

"She's acting like a goat," Matt said, "pushing others around when she thinks she can get away with it." Wow, our new life had made him a philosopher!

"Let's cool down because this is all going to blow over," Frank said.

We scattered to unpack our boxes. As the house fell silent, a shrill goat sound pierced my ears. I heard it again and again, and after trying to ignore it for a while, I went out to ask Buck about it.

"Oh yeah, those two kids. I've been meaning to take care of it. I'll do it this week."

"Take care of it? What does that mean?" It sounded horrible.

"A simple training method. You give the goat your undivided attention, and the second it stops making noise, you give it a raisin. It goes back to making noise out of habit, but you keep watching for the split second when it stops and reward that. A raisin really gets their attention because it's a big spurt of calories compared to their coarse natural diet. They learn to stop crying because their brain is motivated to repeat any behavior linked to a reward. But it takes time, and I've been busy getting the place ready for the Jaynes family. Today, it's at the top of my list."

"I'm confused. Is the noise natural or not?"

"It's the natural alarm call of baby goats, but their sense of alarm is learned. These twins learned it because their mother had a difficult delivery, so she didn't feed them for a while. They kept calling and that wired in the habit. Don't worry, we feed them if the mother can't, but we don't rush it because that undermines nature. We set a timer and their mom fed them in less than three hours."

"That's fascinating. What would happen in nature without your raisins?"

"Mom would bite them when they cry because the noise attracts predators. The little nip teaches them fast."

"Andrea would love to learn to train them. Can she help you sometime?"

"Sure. We can even do it now if she's free."

"I'll send her out!"

Soon enough, the noise stopped and Andrea walked into the house with a huge smile. I decided to reward her for doing this. Of course, the activity is its own reward, but I wanted to solidify the habit so it would last when the novelty was over. What could I give her that's as valuable as a raisin is to a goat?

"Andrea, a second-grade class is coming here to learn about goats tomorrow."

"That's so cool! I want to be there!"

"You have school."

"Can't I miss one class? I really want to see this."

"Sure. As long as your boxes are unpacked."

4
Self-Restraint

On Monday morning, our boots were ready and we ran out as soon as we heard the school kids. Their excitement was indeed a pleasure, as was Miss Robin's age-appropriate biology lesson.

While she was explaining goat digestion, two goats started butting heads. It was quite dramatic, so all attention shifted to that.

"Why are they fighting?" a student asked.

"I can explain," I said, walking to the front of the class. "They are fighting for the best spot in front of the food. They have more food than they need here, but their natural impulse is to grab the best spot in any situation if they are strong enough. Maybe you've seen someone do that on the playground? Maybe you've seen a baby grab a toy from another baby even though there are plenty of other toys. You've learned not to push and grab probably. But it takes work to control that impulse because it's natural mammalian programming."

By now, a different pair of goats started tussling. One reared up on its hind legs and then the other did. The kids' attention was riveted.

"Why don't you stop them?" a student said.

I grabbed a bucket and turned it upside down and stood on top so they could all hear me. "Goats lived in nature long before they lived on farms. No one gives them food in nature and they have to work hard to get enough to eat. Sometimes they get very hungry so they get very pushy. Maybe you remember being very hungry one day and you just wanted to grab any food you saw. Of course, you didn't because you used your words instead. Goats can't talk, so they just push when they really want something."

The goats kept stealing the show with a head-butt here and a side-shove there.

"Will they get hurt?" a kid shouted out.

The kids clustered around me to listen, and in the process, one accidentally pushed into another. The kid who got pushed elbowed back, which sparked retaliation. More kids got shoved in the process, and they retaliated too.

"This is what I mean. When you feel pushed, you want to push back, and that leads to more pushing. We learn to restrain the urge to push, but it's not easy. So when you feel like pushing, tell yourself 'I'm not a goat.' Let's try it. When I say three, everyone take a step back, and if you get bumped by someone, just say: 'I'm not a goat.' Ready? One. Two. Three."

They did it! They spaced themselves out beautifully without a conflagration. Miss Robin jumped in at this moment. "Thank you. Our time is limited so let's move on to the milking barn."

Buck led the way and I went back to Andrea and Bunnie. I was glad they'd been there to hear my stump speech, and glad Suzi wasn't. I always seemed to be scanning for her with my mammalian predator detector.

That night at dinner, we told Frank and Matt all about it.

Andrea said, "Where did you get all that, Mom?"

"Psychology was my undergraduate major, and I was an intern at the zoo in grad school. But a lot of it came from nature videos. I love them and we haven't watched in a while. Want to have a nature video festival tonight?"

"I'll make the popcorn," Frank said.

"Sure," the kids said blandly. They couldn't be too enthusiastic about my ideas, but I knew they couldn't resist because I didn't invite them to watch TV often.

Andrea got upset at the sight of a gazelle being eaten alive. She ran out of the room, but came back soon, and even stayed for the carnivores episode. It showed how a lion misses in 95% of its chases, and sometimes doesn't eat for a week. By the end of the episode, she was rooting for the lion.

"Buck should watch this," she said. "It explains why goats are so fearful."

"It explains why people are fearful too," I said.

5

Visitations

On Tuesday, I heard voices as I woke up. The noise came from outside, I realized, and rushed to the window. There was a crowd holding signs that said "Stop Cruelty to Goats." Frank rushed up behind me.

"What is this?" he said.

"I bet Suzi is involved" I groaned.

Frank called the police. They said they couldn't stop the protest, but they came to clear our driveway so we could get out. They stopped to chat with the protesters, who were apparently eager to share. A couple of them mentioned getting Continuing Education Units from their addiction recovery program for their "work" on this "action." One said she needed the credit to graduate from a court-mandated program to clean a drug-related offense off her record.

Frank and I were furious, but we didn't know what to do.

"What's the name of that place where Suzi works?" Frank said.

"Let's not fan the flames yet. Maybe this will burn out." We tried to distract the kids from the scene as we rushed them off to school.

On Wednesday morning, we awoke to loud honking sounds. We rushed to the window and saw two cars honking at each other as they went for the same parking spot. Both drivers inched forward until they almost touched. Finally, one moved on to another parking spot a few feet away. Then, each driver rushed to the protest with a Goat-Cruelty sign in their hand. Suzi must be deducting points for lateness, I thought.

Frank froze in horror. Finally, he said, "If this happened to one of my clients, I'd tell them to apologize and then send a big bill. But I can see that apologies would just be red meat for our predator." He rushed off to work to discuss it with his partner, while I discussed it with the kids.

"Why do they hate us?" Andrea said.

"Why are they stupid?" Matt said. He ran to the front door to take videos of them. I wanted to reassure him that it would all blow over, but I didn't find that convincing myself. While I debated what to do, my phone buzzed. It was Miss Robin.

"Mrs. Jaynes, I'm calling to warn you that our Principal will be inviting you to her office."

"P-p-p-p-principal's office?" As a proud grown up with real-life problems, I couldn't imagine those words unnerving me, but they did.

"Yes. She observed my students behaving unusually well yesterday and asked me what happened. I thought you should tell her yourself." She sounded cold, but I assumed she was just formal.

"Nice! Thanks for letting me know."

Principal Rodolfo's call came soon after. I suggested that she come to the farm to have the information in context, and she agreed. I agreed to 4pm, feeling sure the protestors would be gone by then.

The kids and I left for our respective schools and the protestors expressed themselves to an empty house.

At 4pm, I turned on the teapot and the doorbell rang right on time.

"I'm Tania Rodolfo," the Principal said. "Just call me Rodolfo. Everyone does."

I brought a teapot onto the deck overlooking the goatyard, and repeated my words from Monday. Rodolfo was so excited that she stood up and applauded. "We have tried to teach self-control for decades and nothing... well... this is a welcome change. Next Monday, we have a teacher-training. Would you come and repeat this?"

"Sure. Would you like to host it here so the teachers can get a visceral feeling for mammalian impulses?"

"Thank you! That's exactly what I was hoping for. We sure can't bring the goats to school! The janitors union would block it since it's not in the contract."

Just then, my husband got home from work. He saw us on the deck and ran toward us. He picked me up and twirled me in the air, something he'd never done before. While twirling, he whispered in my ear "We got a court injunction to stop the protest!" I didn't know what an injunction is, but the word "stop" was all I needed to hear.

Rodolfo stared and then broke into a smile. "We should have you speak at the Sex Education workshop too."

6

Broadcast

Friday morning the street was quiet, but we'd been conditioned to rush to the window as soon as we woke up. We saw that the protesters were on the other side of the street, in apparent respect of the 50-foot ruling. Next to them was a van with a satellite dish and the logo of a local news station. The van had a big cord leading to a big microphone, which was covering the big mouth of our neighbor Suzi. Behind her, protesters chanted and waved signs in unison for the camera. A hand-held loudspeaker led them in a chorus of: "Save - The - Goats."

I shrieked and the kids came running. I was speechless, but Frank said, "Never negotiate with terrorists." I tried to lighten the mood by chattering about our branding meeting on Saturday.

Then Buck knocked on the back door. "Mrs. Jaynes…"

"Please, call me Claire."

"Claire, Bunnie and I admire the way your family has turned the other cheek, but we wonder when you will run out of cheeks."

I was thrilled to discuss this with him since we were out of ideas. So as everyone else left to start their day, I sat down for tea with Buck.

"I feel a bit responsible for this mess," he said, "since I ran my big mouth at our neighbor. But no law says I have to agree with someone, right?"

"It may depend on the size of their horns," I said. "But we don't blame you at all. We blame the animal urge to defend one's turf, whether it's physical turf or ideological turf."

"Glad to hear that. You know, Bunnie and I have lived next to Madame for a decade, and we thought you might be interested in the background. When she first moved into the neighborhood, she'd inspect our garbage when I brought it to the curb. Then she'd knock on our door and tell us that we were doing it wrong. At first we honored her suggestions, but she just came more often and found more to criticize. Bunnie had the ladylike idea of being nice to her. She offered her muffins and coffee, and Suzi just sat there critiquing Bunnie's kitchen. So my darling wife brought a batch of muffins to her house. I said, 'Bunnie, if you give a goat a treat when it head-butts, it will do more head-butting.' So we started being polite to Madame, but no more."

"I appreciate hearing that a lot."

"About the protests," he said, "I just don't have a solution." We hung our heads.

"Bunnie is planning to bring you more muffins tomorrow morning," he added.

I had an idea. "Can Bunnie make biscuits?"

"Of course."

I was excited to put my plan into action, so I said goodbye and graded a stack of papers so I'd be free to pick up Andrea after school. I asked her to help me with a surprise. We went shopping for goat cheese at a few local stores so we could have a cheese tasting at our Saturday meeting. It would be delicious on Bunnie's homemade biscuits. It wouldn't exactly solve the problem, but it would keep our spirits up for one more day.

It was fun to browse the cheese counter of each local store. Suddenly, I really understood goat browsing. They are scanning alternatives and choosing the best way to meet their needs.

The checkout lines were long, so I called Frank to tell him we'd be late for dinner. I heard him muffle a groan, and then whisper to someone. He said goodbye, and I felt a sense of dread about what I would find when I got home.

The line barely moved, so I distracted myself from my sense of foreboding by suggesting to Andrea that we research goat browsing. We pulled out our phones, and in a minute, she told me that wild goats need to forage all day to get enough nutrition. They eat a wide range of plants, but they're choosy. They eat their favorites first and then go back to their less preferred options.

"I wonder how they decide," I said. I kept searching and discovered that dopamine plays a big role. According to Professor Breuning, dopamine is released when the mammal brain sees a way to meet a need. That motivates forward action and releases energy to fuel the action. Suddenly, I understood humans. We find other ways to spark dopamine because we don't need to forage all day like our ancestors did. We keep finding new needs to meet to keep stimulating the joy of dopamine. I explained this to Andrea as we loaded our groceries into the car.

"How do we know what will spark our dopamine?" Andrea asked.

"Good question," I said. It was the ultimate question of life, I thought, so I searched a bit more before turning on the car. "Prof. Breuning says that we look for ways to spark the social chemicals, oxytocin and serotonin. When we know what sparks these chemicals in animals, our own drives make sense."

Andrea didn't push me to turn on the car, so I kept reading aloud. "The animal brain rewards you with the good feeling of serotonin when you have a moment of social dominance. It rewards you with oxytocin when you find social protection. These social rewards help you do what it takes to keep your genes alive, so we've inherited a brain that seeks them." Wow. Not what I was taught, but so obviously true. I wish I knew all this when I was Andrea's age.

Loretta Breuning

7
A Toast

When we got home, we were stunned to see the candlelight dinner that Frank and Matt had prepared. They used goat cheese in every course! I cried with joy at this gesture of hope in the face of our inscrutable challenge.

We dug into the goat appetizers, and Matt asked a great question. "Why do people always say 'wine and cheese,' like you need to eat cheese with wine? It limits who can buy our cheese."

"Matt, that's brilliant!" Frank said. "You solved our branding problem!"

"What did I say?"

"Goat cheese is usually positioned as you said, so if we position ours differently, we'll have less competition."

"Goat cheese for kids!" Andrea said.

"That's it!" Frank said. "Goat cheese is usually combined with flavors that don't appeal to kids, like garlic and rosemary and even ashes, so we can make new combinations." Before we could react, there was a knock at the back door.

It was Bunnie with a plate of biscuits. "Sorry to interrupt. I never imagined you'd be having a candlelight dinner. I wanted to bring these now because I'm going out in the morning. My daughter-in-law is bringing me to a goat yoga class. She thought I'd like it. I can't imagine liking fake goat interactions when I can have real ones, but I decided to just be grateful."

"Interesting," Frank said, and jumped up to grab his laptop. "Where is this goat yoga?"

Bunnie told him and he pulled up the page.

"It looks cheesy," Matt said, looking over Frank's shoulder.

"They spelled cheese wrong" Andrea said.

"No, that's 'chi,' not 'cheese.' They're saying that goat yoga will raise your 'chi,'" I explained.

"What's chi?" said Andrea. Frank explained.

"That sounds cheesy" Matt quipped again.

Frank and I looked at each other. "That's it!" he said.

"That's the name of the cheese!" I said. I got a marker and paper and wrote "Chi-Z" in big letters.

We loved it! I wanted to celebrate with a toast, so I opened a bottle of sparkling apple cider and poured a flute for everyone. We stood and clinked, "To Chi-Z!"

When the excitement passed and we sat down, Frank announced that Matt made dessert.

"Dad wanted me to make goat creme brûlée, but I thought it sounded gross" he said. "So I designed a dessert that I would like." He brought out a plate of colorful little food sculptures. It was a work of art.

"Goat Petit Fours," I said.

"What's that?" Matt said.

"It's French for 'little baked things,'" I explained.

"But I didn't bake them," Matt insisted. "I mixed goat cheese with jam and heavy cream and spread it onto almond crackers, and decorated the top with fruit and nuts" I bit in and it truly was amazing, even if I weren't his mother.

We invited Bunnie to join in our dessert, and she called Buck to join too. Then I had an idea. I stood up with my glass and said "Forty teachers are coming here on Monday. Let's serve them Goat Petit Fours!"

Frank said stood up with his glass and said, "Let's make them with Chi-Z Goat Cheese!" We laughed. It was the much-needed laugh of people who are afraid of what tomorrow morning will bring.

Buck and Bunnie exchanged looks. "The timing is tight," Buck said.

"But we can do it," Bunnie insisted.

Buck pulled a pad and pencil from his pocket and did math out loud as he wrote. He mumbled numbers for milk flow and cheese yield and portion size. "No problem, we can do it!"

"I'll cancel the goat yoga so we can start tomorrow," Bunnie said with a giggle.

"I'll mix the cheese with jam and cream," Matt said.

"I'll arrange the fruit on top," Andrea said.

"I'll tell Rodolfo that we'll provide a snack."

"Bunnie, have you made goat cheese before?" Frank asked.

"Of course. I made it a lot once I heard that goat milk is healthier than cow milk. That's how Buck came to work for your uncle. We came here to buy goat milk fifteen years ago and they got to talking."

We went to bed feeling good that night.

8

Mammals

On Saturday morning, no protestors were outside our window. What a relief. Frank and I resisted the urge to check the news, or scan for Suzi, or speculate on the future. We were glad to have our Chi-Z meeting to distract us. We held it on our back porch so we could watch the goats while we talked.

"The next step is to design a logo," Frank said.

Suddenly we noticed that Matt's chair was empty. He was there a minute ago. "Maaaatt?"

"I'm here," he shouted from behind the refrigerator door. "Keep going, I can hear you." He was spreading jam and goat cheese onto a biscuit.

"Matt, you did it again!" Frank said. "You've targeted our market niche. Instead of peanut butter and jelly sandwiches, kids can bring goat cheese and jelly sandwiches to school."

"It's a portable breakfast alternative to boring egg sandwiches," I added.

With this inspiration, we came up with a logo that looked like a goat flying on a baguette. "This will work!" Frank said. "Now we have to scale."

"What's that?" Matt asked.

"It's a math problem," Frank explained. "We figure out what it costs to make the cheese and what we can sell it for. We'll need a lot of details, so let's divide into teams. Matt and Andrea can go to Bunnie and Buck and write down every step of what they do so we can estimate our costs. Mom and I will talk to the shops in town to find out what they would pay and how much they might buy."

"I bet they'll pay a lot!" Andrea said, mirroring our optimism.

"Andrea, you're old enough to learn about retail mark-up," Frank said. "If you buy a cheese for ten dollars, the store keeps five dollars.

"And the farmer spends a lot to get the goat milk and transport the cheese," I added. "We risk losing money on every sale if we're not careful."

"And if we make any profit, the government will take half," Frank said.

"Geeeeeeez," said Matt. "I thought this would be fun." He hung his head, and Andrea hung hers.

"This is a good way to learn that success is usually harder than it appears. Should we tell them about liability, Frank?"

"Let's save that for next Saturday," he said, and hung his head too. We all kept dipping into our reserves of optimism.

On Sunday, we rented folding chairs and spruced up the goatyard to be ready for the teachers. The protestors seemed to have weekends off, but we lived in fear of Monday.

Fortunately, the street was all quiet that morning. The teachers arrived happily because this was more fun than their usual mandatory trainings. I repeated my talk about mammalian social rivalry, standing the bucket as before. Then I added a new topic.

"Teaching excites me because of the memorable moment when I got to teach a goat. I was an intern at the zoo during grad school, and they put me in the training program that all volunteers take. That included a chance to participate in a goat training. The zookeepers trained a goat to walk across a seesaw by rewarding it with a raisin for each step forward. Then I got to do it myself."

"My goat ran up the seesaw to get the treat, but when it got to the top, the seesaw wobbled and it froze in terror. It wouldn't move, so I brought the raisin closer. It just stared for a while, and then it suddenly took a timid step to get the raisin. Then another step to get another reward. Within seconds, it marched to the bottom and began another climb. This time it practically flew across the seesaw. It had clearly learned to trust its own skills. Soon, one raisin was all it took to motivate a whole seesaw circuit. I was amazed to see how the mammal brain learns to manage fear to get a reward."

Then I led a discussion that gradually flowed toward the fact that teachers are mammals and we're all challenged to manage our mammal brain.

The reactions were not all positive. To be honest, I saw long faces on half the teachers, including Miss Robin. I took it personally for a while, and then Rodolfo pulled me aside. "Do you understand that you are contradicting their professional training?"

"How? What's controversial about managing impulses?"

"The prevailing paradigm of Teacher Education is that children's natural impulses are all good, so they should not be repressed in any way. This is a corollary to the belief that all bad impulses are caused by our society, so we should change society instead of holding a person responsible."

I was shocked. "Does that work? I mean, is it conducive to education?"

"It works for the teacher because we cannot get credentialed and promoted unless we accept the paradigm." I was sad to hear that, but happy to hear Rodolfo's trust in me.

Our goat-cheese treats cut the tension. People asked what it was, and I wished I had a printed flyer with the recipe and the Chi-Z logo. Next time.

When the event ended, I walked people to the exit and I noticed a teacher going straight to Suzi's house. I casually walked next to him and asked if he knew Suzi.

"Yes, I was one of her…um…students. Years ago." I wanted to find out who he was, so I stuck my hand out and said, "Claire Jaynes." He stuck his hand out and said "Jules." Hmmm. Just Jules? I worried about just Jules. Maybe I had seen too many detective shows, because I watched the street for a long time from my window, hoping to catch his license plate. But I had a mountain of preparation for my classes tomorrow, so I slowly let go of it.

9

Predation

Everything returned to normal. Frank caught up on his marketing campaigns and the kids caught up with homework. I caught up on my Marketing lectures and spent free moments visualizing a Chi-Z recipe flyer.

On Thursday morning, I saw a gaggle of protestors when I arrived on campus. A satellite van was near them and a journalist was conducting an interview. As I approached, I was amazed to see that Jules was the person being interviewed. I heard him say, "Professor Jaynes has assaulted human decency and animal decency." The protestors' signs said "Protect Kids & Goats" and "Stop the Attack on Decency."

I ran into the building and texted Rodolfo: "Who is Jules?"

"Professor Jules Caterwaul is Chair of Educational Neuroscience at your university. I invited him to your workshop as a courtesy because he consults for us sometimes. I didn't think he'd come."

I wanted to tell Rodolfo what was happening, but it was too scary to put it into words. So I said, "watch the news."

I sat at my desk but couldn't work. I had to leave for class soon and worried about walking across campus to the lecture hall. Then I realized that no one seemed to recognize me when I walked past the protestors. They don't even know me! It's not personal! They're just paid protestors.

That eased the pain enough for me to ponder J. Caterwaul. Why does he hate me and how is he paying them? Then I reminded myself not to take it personally. He doesn't hate me like a wolf doesn't hate a goat. He's just preying on me to nourish himself. I still felt bad, but strong enough to teach.

I left campus as soon as my two classes were over to avoid unpleasant reminders of the drama de jour. I didn't want to upset the kids so I detoured to Frank's office to tell him privately. He brushed it off as a passing fad. That bothered me, but I probably would have felt worse if he'd been upset. One of us should not feel like prey.

On Friday, I woke up with a sense of dread, but my phone pinged before I could scan for threat signals.

A text from Rodolfo said, "Great news. Some teachers reported a good response to your method. One was so excited that she persuaded the Superintendent of Schools to have a district-wide teacher training. How many can you host?"

"How many do you have?" I replied.

"160"

"Wow. Fabulous! Can do. When?"

"In four weeks."

I rushed to tell Buck and Bunnie. "We need to do it for 160 people in four weeks. What do you think?"

Buck whipped out the tiny memo pad that dated him to a bygone era. "Let's see. We can seat 80 in one barnyard while serving snacks to the rest in the other barnyard. Both groups would have a view of the goats the whole time."

"Brilliant!" I said.

I went back to grab Frank before he left for work, and in my excitement, I babbled about the urgent need for a recipe flyer.

He was right on top of it. "It would need to include our website, so I'll prepare one. And we'll need signage to call attention to the flyers. I'll draft something and we can work on it at our Saturday meeting." His optimism frustrated me yesterday, but now it felt good.

I sat in my home office to grade a stack of papers, but my mind kept drifting to this Caterwaul person. I started searching and was surprised to find that he was a big man on campus. He led a prestigious research project that provided paid internships for many students. That was the coin of the realm at my school. But where did the money come from? I bet Suzi knew, but it wasn't worth the risk of landing in her crosshairs.

Frank's thoughts were flowing in a similar direction. Instead of driving to his office, he went to my campus to see if the protestors were there. A call came in a few minutes. "Are you sitting? Four news vans are here – the local station, two national affiliates, and one unmarked. It's upsetting, but I thought you should know."

10

Support

Now, I was upset. I had restrained myself long enough. I wanted to butt their heads.

Better to vent with someone who could help me make sense of this insanity. I thought of Rodolfo and rushed to her office without warning.

"No, I don't have an appointment," I told the school secretary. "Yes, I'll take a seat."

When the secretary stepped away, I barged into Rodolfo's office and reported the news. Fortunately, she did understand.

"Some teachers here objected to your training, but we get objections to everything so I didn't dwell on it."

"I don't see why they'd object if it got good results."

"They say you went about it the wrong way."

"Why is there a right way and a wrong way?"

"Because the teacher-training scriptures instruct us to obey the theory and excommunicate heretics."

"So they're basically protecting their turf."

"Your method creates a lot of cognitive dissonance."

"I don't see why you call it my method. I thought it was Psychology 101. Doesn't everyone know that the brain learns from rewards?"

"The high priests of Teacher Education have decreed that extrinsic rewards are evil. Learning is its own reward according to their theory."

"That sounds nice, but what about kids who don't love to learn?"

"We're supposed to blame society and we're never supposed to question the theory. Unfortunately, the theory overlooks the huge reward value of attention. A kid can get more attention by not learning than by learning. Each rewarding moment wires the brain to seek more rewards in that way, so rejecting learning becomes a habit."

"Power is a huge reward too. You only get a moment of power when you reject learning, but it's easy to see how tempting that would be to a young mammal. It's sad to imagine young brains getting wired to reject learning."

"That's why it's so useful for people to hear you say that reward learning is natural. Education should work with nature, but we work against it when we make reward learning taboo."

"Where did this crazy theory come from?"

"I blame Rousseau. Almost three hundred years ago, he sold the idea that nature is all good, so everything bad comes from society. He's behind the illusion that animals are all good, children are all good, and hunter-gatherers were all good. He ignores the aggression of animals, children and hunter-gatherers, so we learn to ignore it too. We're trained to blame it on society instead of seeing that it's natural."

"Wow, you're right. We filter reality through the lens of that theory. No one actually lived with animals would believe that. In Rousseau's time, most people lived with animals, but cities were growing. So his theory grew, and today most people live far enough from nature to believe the warm and fuzzy view."

"We can do something about this. The Superintendent asked me to draft the invitation for the district-wide workshop. Why don't we work on it now?"

"With pleasure." I suddenly realized that staying busy was helping me more than raging would.

"The Superintendent is aware of the mixed vibes, so let's be cautious. Humans won't be motivated by raisins, so how can we make it real?"

"Let's explain our natural reward chemicals – dopamine, serotonin, and oxytocin. They're released when you meet a need, and our brain defines that with neural pathways built from its own past experience. People need to know that happy chemicals are like paving on your neural pathways, so we're all tempted to repeat behaviors that sparked good feelings in our past."

"Where did you learn this?"

"From Professor Breuning. It makes so much sense that I wondered how I missed it in school, but now I see that no schools are teaching this."

"Let's not mention that."

"The resistance to this basic biology has surprised me. I think it's because our conscious verbal brain wants to believe it's in charge. It's uncomfortable to think that our non-verbal brain controls the emotional chemicals."

"When you say 'emotional chemicals,' you remind me that we should talk about stress chemicals too."

"For sure. Threat chemicals create learning just like reward chemicals. They pave neural pathways that help an animal avoid predators faster in settings where their alarm bells were triggered in the past. This is why humans are so quick to fear anything linked to a threat from their past. A kid can get wired to fear studying if their threat chemicals were triggered in the context of studying in their past. They need help to rewire this or they'll keep fearing schoolwork without knowing why."

"Teachers should know this. It's such a shame that they're stuck in the Rousseauian theory that children are born wise."

"Why do they care more about theory than children's futures?"

"They care about keeping their jobs. Loyalty to the herd is rewarded and the theory unites the herd."

"And it feels true because it's rewarded. That's the weird thing about our two-part brain."

"I've been thinking about another reason for the resistance. Mammal groups always have a status hierarchy, and in the modern human world, moral superiority is the preferred way to raise your status. Teachers really need that moral superiority because they don't make a lot of money. They base their sense of superiority on their view that children are born wise. So if you challenge that view, they will not be happy."

"I've been thinking about another reason. Mammals prefer to spread out when they eat and it takes a common enemy to unite them. Human groups always unite by focusing on a common enemy. Rousseau's theory makes society the enemy. Attacking society is a convenient way for a group to keep itself together."

"A goat who's separated from the herd is quickly eaten by a wolf, so I can see why teachers would fear questioning the theory. Safety in numbers is naturally tempting."

"This is helping me a lot. I can't take it personally when I see how natural it is."

"I'd be upset if protesters were outside my office. I'm sorry you're having this extra dose of mammalian behavior. I hope you don't hold it against all teachers. Those Professors of Education are the source of this. They live in a fantasy world because they're never in a classroom full of children."

"Hey, you've just given me a great idea! Are you free tomorrow afternoon? I want to take you to the source."

I called my old mentor at the zoo and he agreed to meet us there the next day. It was the perfect way to lift my spirits.

11

Rewards

At dinner, I didn't mention the protest because I didn't want to upset the kids. Once they left the table, Frank stared at me.

"What?" I said.

"Four media vans in front of your office and you don't want to talk about it? I think it's time to get a lawyer. You didn't answer my messages for an hour so I went ahead and called one."

"Frank, that's crazy! We'll hemorrhage money and go bankrupt and have nothing to show for it. Please, let's give it more time."

"So you propose doing nothing?"

I told him about my talk with Rodolfo and about Teacher Education and the mammalian brain. That didn't relieve his concern, so I tried a different tack. "I've never proposed to do nothing before, right? I usually want to make a plan, right? So just this once, let's say the plan is to do nothing, for a few days. Okay?"

"Okay, just a few days. I'll call the lawyer's voicemail and tell him to ignore my prior message."

"I hope they don't charge us for processing your messages."

Saturday morning, our Chi-Z meeting hammered out plans for the big school-district event. Then I left for the zoo while Frank and the kids worked on the website.

My mentor, Doug Kovich, was waiting at the entrance. I introduced him to Rodolfo as the zoo's marketing genius. "I got my start in marketing by working for him," I said. "But more important, what you call my 'method' comes from one single sentence that Kovich said to me here long ago."

"What is it?" they both chirped.

"The zoo's training program taught us that animals kill their own kind in a wide range of circumstances. A zookeeper would lose their job if they let an animal get killed, so they take pains to protect animals from potential violence, even as they give lip service to the peace-and-love view of animals.

"For example?" Rodolfo asked.

"When a zoo gets a new animal," Kovich said, "zookeepers know it might get killed if they just put it in with an existing group. So they have detailed protocols for these 'introductions.' They put the new animal in a separate enclosure where the existing group can see it, and monitor for aggression. They reward an animal the moment it stops an aggression gesture. But sometimes the aggression continues so the separate enclosure becomes permanent."

"I was always fascinated by the euphemisms that zookeepers create to disguise the true reason for their violence-prevention measures."

"Like what?" Rodolfo asked.

"When zookeepers feed a group, they know that the dominant individual will prevent the others from eating. To be sure that weaker individuals don't starve, they do feedings in pairs. One keeper feeds the dominant individual continually while the other feeds the rest of the group. They call this 'cooperative feeding,' which they rationalize by saying that the alpha is 'cooperating' with them. This fits the peace-and-love view of animals but it completely misrepresents what is going on."

"Fascinating," Rodolfo said.

"So what's the one sentence that shaped you?" Kovich asked.

"They gave us a graduation when we completed the training and the head zookeeper came to speak. She said flowery things about the empathy of animals and I whispered to you, "Does she believe this stuff?" And you said, "She believes it, but she doesn't act on it. You helped me see how often our beliefs and actions don't match, as if we have two separate brains."

"Yes!" he said. "But you left out an important word. First, I said 'Shhhhhh.'"

"How could I forget? That word showed me the tabooness of noticing the gap between beliefs and actions."

"Zookeepers respond to their reward structure like any other mammal," Kovich said. "They are rewarded for promoting the idealized view of animals, but they are also rewarded for results – keeping the animals healthy."

"At least zookeepers aren't pressured to act on false beliefs like teachers are. Wow - now I see why you brought me here!"

"I'm so glad you get it," I said. "Life suddenly made sense to me when I realized that animals can't talk so our animal brain can't tell our human brain what it's reacting to. So our verbal brain just invents things that make us look good."

"Do you think people are powerless over their emotions?" Rodolfo said.

"Not at all. Just that the power is more limited than your verbal brain realizes, so you have to use it strategically. You squander the power when you're busy lying about what's going on."

"If zookeepers lied to themselves about reality, they'd have dead animals immediately, but when teachers lie to themselves about reality, the bad consequences come much later. So there's no consequences for the teachers, or even the professors who forced the theory onto the teachers."

"Shhhhh" Kovich said.

We all laughed. We became a herd facing a common enemy, and it did indeed feel good. But like all happy chemicals, it passed quickly and our attention shifted back to threat signals.

"The problem seems too big to fix by handing out raisins," Rodolfo said.

"I think we'll help a lot by handing out the facts. A big one is the mammalian urge for social dominance. Each brain expresses it with neural pathways wired by its own experience. So one child might express it by striving for good grades while another by fighting on the playground."

"And another by disrespecting the teacher," Kovich said. "I did that when I was young, I'm ashamed to say."

"So if teachers understand our natural reward system they can steer kids toward healthy ways to spark it. Instead of just focusing on formal rewards like grades, we need to understand rewards from the animal brain's perspective."

"That's a big challenge," Kovich said. "Raisins would have motivated my grandparents because they grew up with hunger. Freedom from hunger is relatively new for humanity, so our incentive structures haven't caught up. Kids know they won't starve if they don't do their schoolwork, and that makes it very tempting to be a smart mouth. Speaking from personal experience."

"Rewarding bad behavior creates more bad behavior, said Rodolfo, "so we need to save rewards for good behavior. We fail to do that for so many reasons, alas.

"Parents need to know this as much as teachers," I added.

"If zookeepers reward bad behavior, the consequences are immediately obvious," Kovich said, "but if parents and teachers reward bad behavior, the consequences may not visible for a long time."

"I'm still stuck on the 'shhhhh,'" said Rodolfo. "I wonder what will happen if I say this in public."

"We'll find out in a few weeks," I said.

12

Herd Behavior

On Monday morning, I got a call from my boss, the Chair of the Marketing Department. "What did you do to annoy those Teachers Ed people?"

"It's a long epistemological story. Want to hear it?" I knew he'd say he was too busy. I knew he wasn't really upset about the protest because he waited until Monday to call about it.

"No time now. I'm just calling because the Dean told me to check on it. I have to get back to her now since she called last Friday."

"Just say it's a long epistemological story."

"Nice. I'm good if you're good" he said and hung up. He didn't mention if the protesters were back. And I didn't ask because I wouldn't be able to work if they were. Better to focus on what I have control over, like preparing lectures. When I needed a break, I did some research on making goat cheese.

On Tuesday morning, protestors were there, but media vans were not. I decided to enter the front door of my building, though it meant walking past the protestors. On the way, I heard a voice say: "Isn't that the prof who said the bad stuff?"

I walked faster, but could still hear the reply: "I'm not sure. Should we get her?"

I ran into the building without looking back. I was scared, so I called the campus police. They said no crime had been committed, so they couldn't do anything.

I discussed it with Frank that night. "You shouldn't have to go in the back door. I hate to let them intimidate us. Let's walk in the front door together tomorrow." And that's how Frank ended up in the emergency room of our local hospital. It happened so fast. A guy lunged toward me. Another guy tried to stop him, and the two of them crashed into my non-violent spouse. Frank landed on the pavement face first. He insisted that it wasn't bad, so I drove him to Emergency instead of calling an ambulance.

A nurse asked what happened while she was patching him up. We told her the whole story and asked her opinion on why anyone would protest my goat trainings.

"This hospital feels like a goatyard sometimes," she said. "I have an idea. My nurses' group is scheduled for an in-service training next week and our speaker cancelled. They would love to hear you talk about mammalian impulses."

"I'd be happy to do it. And if you want to have the training in our goatyard to see the mammal brain in action, we'd be happy to host it."

"I'd love to. I'll contact our group leader and get back to you tonight."

"Great. You can sample our goat cheese too."

Frank decided to work at home for the rest of the day rather than show up at the office with a barroom-brawl face. But when we got home, he realized that he was in too much pain to do real work. So he started drafting the Chi-Z website and soon forgot the pain.

On Thursday morning, I decided to check in with my Department Chair before showing up on campus. "No protestors," he said. "I hope you're not making a big deal of this, Jaynes. Students are always getting stirred up. That's the Ed biz."

I wanted to tell him he was wrong – that the brain learns from carrots and sticks, and since sticks became taboo, students seek carrots in dysfunctional ways. I didn't say that because he'd just recite the scriptures and I'd already heard them enough.

A few minutes later, Rodolfo called in a panic. "The protestors are here! Outside the Superintendent's office. His address was on the envelope of the Goat Day invitations."

"Goat Day. I like that!" I didn't mean to sound so happy in her moment of distress. "How can I help?"

"The Superintendent asked to see me right away. I'm on my way there but I'm not sure what to say."

"What we said at the zoo is perfect. Everyone benefits from getting real about the mammal brain."

"That may not calm him down. Who are these goat protestors anyway?"

"We've been asking ourselves that for weeks."

"Weeks? This has been going on for weeks? Why aren't you doing something?"

"I didn't know what to do. But you've given me an idea. Can you come to the goatyard for an emergency meeting?"

"I'll be there right after the Superintendent grills me."

When she arrived, I gave her a muffin and launched into my plan. "We need to figure out where the compensation is coming from. We know that one protestor was compensated with participation units by my neighbor Suzi. My guess is that the others are compensated too. We don't know how, but I suspect Professor Caterwaul is involved since he spoke to the media for the protestors and he funds a lot of student internships. And we know there's a connection between Suzi and Caterwaul because I saw him walking there after your training here."

"Why would Caterwaul be doing this?"

"I've been wanting to research him, but I kept stopping myself to avoid personalizing things. You've convinced me that the time has come. But I thought you might dig up more on him since you're in the Education field."

"I don't know him, but I'll help you research."

My phone rang. It was Nurse Nadia, so I had to take it.

"How many people can you fit?" she asked. "My husband is a hospital administrator and he wants to send his staff for an in-service training."

"We can host a hundred sixty," I said.

"Good. I'll get back to you tomorrow with more details."

During the call, Rodolfo started searching and then got up to leave. I hung up in time to catch her. "I'm going to snoop around at Caterwaul's office. It's something you can't do since you might be recognized."

"Good idea. I'll do the same for you and snoop at School District Headquarters." On the way there, I realized that I could be recognized if the protestors were the same as the earlier ones. I looked for a way to disguise myself, but all I found in the car was old yoga pants. So I wrapped the pants around my head like a turban, and took photos of the protestors from a distance. After a while, two vans drove up and half the protestors got in. The others scattered on foot after putting their signs in a van. This was a well-orchestrated operation!

The thought of it filled me with fear.

13

Dominance Contest

I staggered to my car and locked the doors. Fear stabbed me the whole way home as I imagined an orchestrated operation aimed at me. This was not irrational fear, I told myself. It was rational to feel like a goat facing a wolf pack.

In nature, a goat runs at the first whiff of threat. Fear exists for a good reason: it motivates fast action that helps you survive. Fear chemicals do their job by making you feel so bad that you do what it takes to make them stop. My fear chemicals stopped when I thought about quitting the goat talks. I didn't want to quit, but the relief from fear felt so good.

My verbal brain started looking for excuses to quit. These goat talks don't pay the bills. They don't get applause. They take too much time. The "rational" brain is always rationalizing to help the emotional brain get what it wants.

I thought about calling Rodolfo to cancel. Then I conjured up her response. She would be shocked and I would feel shame. I thought about going ahead with her workshop and then stopping. That relieved my fear long enough for me to catch my breath. I collapsed onto the lounge chair overlooking the goat yard. Why not just enjoy this instead of inviting the whole world to tramp through, I thought.

But I still felt shame at the thought of quitting. I could blame Rodolfo for shaming me in this imagined conversation, but I knew enough about the brain to know that I was doing it to myself.

What did I have to be ashamed of? Couldn't I feel proud without these workshops?

Before I could answer, Andrea got home. She stood next to me without saying anything. I finally broke the silence. "How was your day?"

"Are you OK?" she said.

"Sure. Why wouldn't I be OK?"

"I've never seen you lying on a lounge chair in the middle of the day."

"I've been thinking. Maybe I'll stop doing these goat chats and just focus on the cheese."

She ran to her room and shut the door without saying anything. That's fine, I told myself. To her it was just a party. It's natural for a kid to mourn the loss of parties, but she has her own parties ahead of her.

Soon, Matt came home. We got right to the point.

"I think I'll stop doing these goat chats, so now we'll have time for a family vacation."

"Mom, that's crazy. You're changing the world. Why would you stop?"

I didn't answer so he finally went to his room. Typical teenager. Everything is about changing the world. They don't realize they're just trying to change the status hierarchy so they can move up. Every new generation of mammals will push to establish itself. Matt needs to do that for himself instead of expecting his mother to do it for him.

Then Frank came home. I didn't wait for him to remark on my supine position. "I've been thinking that goat talks are not the best way to market our cheese. We can find a better marketing strategy."

He didn't grab the bait. As much as Frank loves to talk about marketing strategy, he could see there was more on my mind. I told him about the protest at School District Headquarters, and how it was obviously organized and funded. He said we have nothing to fear but fear itself - not in those words, since he's more original. I told him that fear is necessary for survival in a world of predators.

"What are you talking about? I don't see a predator." Then he walked into his office.

I jumped up to follow him, but realized I was too hungry to quibble. I decided to make dinner while thinking things over.

As I started to leave the goat deck, I heard a familiar tap-tap-tap sound. I heard that sound so often that I almost stopped noticing. Sure enough, it was the sound of horns clicking as two goats went at each other. It was a good reminder that social rivalry is part of life for every mammal.

I started browning meat for chili and searched on goat aggression while it cooked. The first page was just the usual talk of male reproductive contests. But as I browned onions and dug into the third page of results, female aggression came up. Apparently, female goats seek dominance when it benefits their kids. They submit when that benefits their kids. Interesting. The onions started to burn.

I mixed all the ingredients and read the websites of some goat farmers while waiting for the chili to bubble. In the comments, real goat farmers shared fascinating experiences with female aggression.

As I stirred the chili, I thought about the natural urge to spread one's genes. Animals don't know what genes are, but their brains reward any behavior that promotes reproduction. Humans don't consciously care about spreading their genes, but we've inherited a brain that rewards us when we compete for mates and protect the young.

The chili bubbled so hard that it made a mess. I thought about the urge for social dominance as I wiped up the mess. I suddenly saw how social dominance helps an animal promote its genes. I was trained to think of dominance-seeking as an evil of our society, but it's really part of nature. All mammals strive for social power in whatever way available to them. Hunter-gatherers strive for social power. Toddlers strive for social power. Adult humans mask the impulse with fancy verbiage, but they still do it relentlessly.

Loretta Breuning

Suddenly, I understood my fear. Losing a dominance contest is a survival threat from the animal brain's perspective. I panicked when I saw an opponent that was bigger than me. How could I relieve this fear?

The smell of chili drew everyone into the kitchen with a lean and hungry look, so I declared that dinner was ready.

When we sat down, Matt said, "I heard about the protest at school."

"I heard about it on the news," Frank said.

"People seem to squabble as much as goats," Andrea said.

"Goats don't squabble all the time," I said. "They size up their rivals and pull back until they think they can win."

That's it! I just needed to size up my adversary the way a goat would. I hadn't done that yet because it seemed paranoid to study your enemy. But now I realized that you have to know what you're up against to make good decisions. My fear came from putting myself in the position of the weaker goat, but maybe I'm not the weaker goat.

"Did you hear me?" Frank said. I hadn't heard him, and I apologized. But I didn't share my thoughts. I finally had a solution I liked and didn't want to subject it to anyone's approval. I was determined to find the clockmaker who wound up these protests, and then find their weakness.

14

Limbic Drives

At dawn on Friday morning, Nadia called. "I hope it's not too early. I'm coming off a night shift and need to sleep, but first my husband wants to talk to you about the training next week."

"I'd love to talk to him about it."

"Can you talk now?"

"Sure. He's welcome to come here and see the goats."

"Nah, he gets goats. He's going into surgery but he can talk now. Do you know the coffee shop in Sagacity Hospital?"

"I can be there in twenty minutes," I said. That left me twelve minutes to drive and park, seven minutes to shower and dress, and one minute to tell Frank and listen to his response. While showering, I planned what to say in that minute, but in my excitement, I may have chosen the wrong strategy.

"Next week!" he said. "You expect us to accommodate 160 healthcare workers next week?"

I had ten seconds to answer and the time evaporated while I searched for words. So I took that as a rhetorical question and left.

While I was driving, a call from Rodolfo came in. "I hope it's not too early," she said. "I just found good news in my inbox and thought you'd want to hear. Three of our teachers were so excited about the improvements in their classrooms that they chatted with teachers in other districts. So I got inquiries from three principals in other districts. Want to put on an event for them?"

"Love to. Let's plan it tomorrow."

Nadia's husband was waiting for me at the entrance to the coffee shop. "I'm Dr. Aziz Kamran," he said holding out his hand. I imagined his hand in someone's guts a few minutes from now. "I like your message. Our people should hear it."

"Thanks," I said, waiting for the "but."

"But we need to offer Continuing Education Units if we want people to come. There's a procedure for that, which you need to straighten out with Marsha Ling. Here's her contact info." He typed and sent. "She'll be expecting you."

"Can I tell you more about the content?"

"Sorry. I'm scheduled. Tell Marsha." He stood up to leave.

I could have let him go, but I felt like I needed informed consent. "Do you know what our paradigm is? There could be objections. We will be acknowledging core limbic drives."

"Why would anyone object to basic biology?" he said, and walked out.

I decided to find this Marsha Ling while I was in the building. It was probably too early for her to be in her office, so I lingered over my tea and muffin. My mind generated images of protestors in front of this hospital. I needed to focus on something else, so I looked for directions to Marsha's office. Human Resources. Eighth floor. I grabbed the half-eaten muffin with one hand and texted "on my way" with the other.

"Yes, I have an appointment," I said to the Human Resources receptionist, and she apparently confirmed that I did. But she still seated me in the waiting room.

As I finished my muffin, I searched for ways to make the limbic system sound less Freudian. I had nothing against Freud, but in the context of old goats, misinterpretation was possible. My search led to Breuning's site once again. It explains how the happy brain chemicals reward everything connected to spreading your genes. This includes everything that helps you compete for a partner or protect your young until they compete for partners. This is why humans obsess over their attractiveness and their children's prospects. From night clubs to parent clubs, happy chemicals reward anything linked to what biologists call "reproductive success." I was glad to have this time in the waiting room.

Ms. Ling came to greet me and I blurted out my enthusiasm for the limbic brain. She showed no interest as she led me to her office. She was interested in the forms we'd need to submit.

She asked me for key learning objectives and expected outcomes. I didn't know the difference between a learning objective and an expected outcome, but I saw her type whatever I said, so I just let it flow.

When she stopped typing, she said "You can hold the event on Wednesday."

"What do you mean?"

"Dr. Aziz cannot schedule an event until I certify it, and that won't be possible until Wednesday."

"Okay, Wednesday it is."

"I'll inform Dr. Aziz and he'll get the invites out."

I called Frank with the news and he surprised me with news of his own. "I just put in for a week's vacation, so I can do everything we need to put the company on a legal footing. I'll register a partnership and file with the FDA. First, I'll promote Bunnie to COO and give her a raise, since we're counting on her for production. So I guess we're good for Wednesday."

The cheese business suddenly looked great to me!

15

Recipes

On Saturday, we sat down to our Chi-Z meeting with more excitement than ever. Frank had designed a recipe flyer complete with a logo, a web link, and an image of the cheese package. He would have it printed by Wednesday so the doctors and nurses could bring home a reminder of our cheese. Just one detail remained: what Chi-Z recipe to put on the flyer. For that, Frank had prepared a nice surprise.

He cued Andrea. "Dad has been teaching me about focus groups. I scheduled a focus group for tomorrow to sample different recipes. I want to practice on you guys now, okay?" Then she tapped her phone and Bunnie appeared at the back door with a platter.

"This is so exciting," I said.

"Be serious, Mom," Matt said.

"How is that not serious?"

"We are going to sample three different goat cheese recipes," Andrea said in a formal tone, "and then we want to hear your opinion of them."

I bit into the first sample and said, "Wow, this is delicious! Can I have the recipe?" Matt scowled, but

Andrea and Bunnie made a note. I curbed my enthusiasm, but all three were delicious.

When it was over, I asked if I could help. Bunnie said yes, please round up five more participants. They had eleven so far, which was too many for one group but not enough for two. They didn't know who else to ask since they'd gone through all of Bunnie's church contacts and Andrea's friend's parents. "Two groups would be more scientific," Andrea added.

I figured I'd invite Rodolfo when she came and ask her to bring someone. Then I called Kovich and left a voicemail asking him to come and bring two guests. That was a pretty sloppy way of rounding up five people, but Rodolfo would soon arrive to work on the teacher workshop. I couldn't wait to hear about her stalking of Caterwaul and tell her about my stalking of the protestors.

She pulled up a photo of a door that said "Caterwaul Lab" and it took my breath away. The enemy suddenly felt tangible.

"Students were constantly going in and out," she said. "I peeked in briefly when the door swung open and didn't see any laboratory equipment. Only a seminar table and computers."

"We have to find out what they're researching and who's funding it."

"First, we need to compose a reply to the three principals who want our workshop. I want to plan a mammal-brain workshop that could run in any school district. It would need more speakers," she said looking down reticently, in case it hurt my feelings. "Maybe a panel of three teachers who got good results. Plus someone with animal experience beyond goats."

"Let's ask Kovich to contact a zookeeper."

"I was hoping you'd say that."

"I phoned him just before you came and he didn't answer, but I know he works on Saturday because it's all-hands-on-deck at the zoo. Why don't we drive over there?"

We found Kovich in front of the chimpanzees. He was holding up a skull and explaining the sagittal crest to a cluster of young families. They asked him where to buy snacks. When he finished, he cordially agreed to find us a zookeeper willing to speak to teachers. He had fascinating commentary as he walked us through the zoo. But each time we passed a zookeeper and invited them, they declined. Kovich felt bad, and agreed to show up at our focus group. Alone.

On Sunday morning, we all pitched in to set up. I volunteered to assemble the goat-cheese petit fours. It was mindless work, so my mind wandered to Caterwaul Lab. What was going on behind that door? I tried to think of something else, but with each petit four I garnished, my urge to stalk Caterwaul got stronger. I resolved to do it as soon as this was over.

The first focus group loved our cheese treats and I loved hearing it. Andrea and Bunnie took lots of notes. As Group 1 left and Group 2 arrived, a little knot of people formed in front of our house. Amidst the sea of faces, I was shocked to see Suzi. Did she think this was an open house? I did not want her dark cloud over this event, despite the empty seats. So I personally escorted Group 2 to make sure it was invitation-only.

I sat on the sidelines while Andrea and Bunnie conducted the conversation. Gazing out the window, I was sure I saw Suzi's head popping up from the fence at our property line. It spoiled the joy of this wonderful moment.

But I recaptured the pleasure when Andrea and Bunnie announced their two perfect recipes for the flyer. Then I was finally free to start my research. But as I walked toward my laptop, I noticed Matt looking glum. He had never been jealous when his sister had the spotlight, so I asked what was wrong.

"Why do they hate you?" he said.

I was tempted to say "no one hates me," but that would be invalidating. And his question was reasonable in the circumstances. It must be hard to see people protest your mother. So I said "Why do you ask?"

"I'm doing homework for this teacher who…who… was one of the protestors. She even talked about it in class."

That bothered me, but I wanted to stay calm for Matt. All I could do was babble about the mammal brain. I explained the intense competition for mates in the animal world, and how that causes crazy emotions in humans. No one can admit that they care about social dominance, so people concoct theories to give themselves moral superiority. He actually seemed interested, so I grabbed his phone and downloaded Prof. Breuning's book, *I, Mammal: How to Make Peace with the Animal Urge for Social Power*.

"If you get upset about the mammalian behavior around you," I continued, "you will be upset forever. Our brain can either focus on threat or reward. If you focus on threat you will always feel bad, and you won't know how you've done it to yourself. So you might as well focus on rewards." We had a good talk, but I never got to research Caterwaul.

16

Social Entrepreneurship

Matt focused on rewards in a way I never expected. He slipped out of the house on Monday morning and texted later that he was studying with a friend. But Rodolfo heard he was at the protest from a teacher who saw him and told another teacher who told another.

I wanted to wait for him to tell me himself, but after a few minutes I couldn't hold back. So I invited him to a sushi lunch, knowing he could never resist. Maybe I was acting as a Chi-Z board member as much as a mother.

As soon as we sat down, he said, "What is social entrepreneurship?"

"Why do you ask?"

"I was only planning to watch the protestors and read their signs," he said. "I hid behind a parked car and wore a hat and a scarf. One of the protesters was a girl who looked my age, so I went over and stood near her. After a while, I said 'Why are you doing this?' And she said 'You mean the social entrepreneurship?' And I said 'yeah,' but I had no idea what it meant."

"How did she answer you?"

"She said there's an undergraduate honors program in Educational Neuroscience that she's trying to get into and this would strengthen her application. Then she asked me why I was doing it, and I said 'It seems like fun.' Such a dumb answer! She frowned at me and said 'You think this is fun?' So what is social entrepreneurship?"

What a tangled web we weave when first we put on a hat and scarf! "Do you know what a euphemism is?"

"Not exactly."

"It's making something sound nice when you know it's not really nice. Entrepreneurship is starting a new business, like we're doing with the cheese. Social entrepreneurship implies that your business is helping others in some way."

"How does a protest start a business or help others?"

"It doesn't. That's why it's a euphemism. She is trying to help herself. A lot of students get internships from Professor Caterwaul. Joining the protest seems like a way to join his herd and get a share of his rewards."

"Why is Caterwaul against us?"

"I keep asking myself that and I keep failing to investigate. Let's do it now." We pulled out our phones and started searching. Matt searched on the name 'Caterwaul', and I thought of great strategy. I went to the home page of my university and searched on the words "social entrepreneurship." Boom. There was a page inviting students to apply for "social entrepreneurship opportunities." It touted a chance to participate in cutting-edge science without specifying further. My jaw dropped.

"Matt, this is it. The professor is using the words himself. He's baiting students with the promise of research funding. But your next class is starting so I'm taking you back."

After school, Matt went straight to his room and shut the door. An hour later, he came out and said, "I did it!" He applied for the "opportunity" at Caterwaul Lab. My boy! "It didn't ask for an essay or anything hard. I didn't give my real name, of course."

The next morning, he slipped out early again and soon sent the message that no protestors were at School District HQ. At the same time, I got a hysterical text from Nadia. "PROTESTORS HERE! Something about goats???"

I called to calm her down, but it went straight to voicemail. I imagined her calling her husband out of surgery. Or getting stonewalled by Ms. Ling in Human Resources. Or maybe spying on the protesters herself.

I wrote to Matt: "Protest moved to hospital. You go to school." Then I sat down to grade papers, but I was too shaken to concentrate, so I went back to researching Caterwaul.

I learned that he was a recognized leader in attention deficit research. His work had been funded by the leading ADHD medication producer for a decade. Two years ago, he was named "Researcher of the Year" by a consortium of pharmaceutical companies. Last year, a competing company awarded him a fellowship with an even bigger research budget. It was enough to hire a lot of students and make him the most popular professor on campus. I'd been too busy with goats and family to follow campus events. Otherwise, I might have noticed Caterwaul's social dominance.

With all that glory, why would he protest goats? His webpage held no clue – only glitz about serving humanity. I postponed the burning question to get to my class on time. I would not be teaching about social entrepreneurship.

17

Reward Learning

In my free hour between lectures, I outlined the presentation I would give to the doctors and nurses. The head-butting of goats would not interest them like school-kids, so I decided to focus on reward learning in goats. I asked Frank to buy raisins and rushed home after class to start training.

It was so much fun that I wished I'd done it sooner. I started with the dance moves that BF Skinner taught his pigeons. You reward a goat each time it turns its head to one side. Keep doing that and the goat soon spins in a full circle in its quest for more raisins. No conscious concept of pirouettes is needed. I was so excited with my spinning goats that I called Bunnie and Buck to show them.

Bunnie wanted to finish sterilizing milk containers, but Buck put down his milking equipment and ran over.

"You may not like the idea of dancing goats," I said, "but isn't it amazing to see how they repeat whatever behavior is rewarded?"

"I'm glad you're doing this because I need to train them to accept medication from a vet and never find the time. Want to help with that?"

"Sure. And that might interest the doctors and nurses I'll be speaking to. Can we bring in Andrea to help?" She was on my mind because she seemed jealous of my sushi lunch with Matt.

We started rewarding goats for stepping onto a scale and tolerating a small prick. But I made a rookie mistake when a goat nudged the pocket where I kept the raisins. I absent-mindedly gave it one, and now it was nudging harder and harder. It was a great reminder of how carefully we must monitor the behavior we are rewarding.

Andrea made a bigger rookie error. She held out a whole handful of raisins instead of a single one. Goats rushed her hand and she dropped the raisins. The goats got a huge reward and Andrea got a lot of bombardment.

Then she made the opposite mistake. She kept all the raisins in her pocket and it took her so long to pull one out that a goat couldn't really tell which behavior was being rewarded. Goats would nudge Andrea's pocket and end up linking the nudge to the reward.

These mistakes were valuable. They'd help us show our healthcare practitioners how easy it is to reward unwanted behavior without intending to.

Frank got home and we set up the seesaw. He showed Andrea how to lure a goat up to the wobbly peak and then motivate it to move through its fear. Buck kept bringing out fresh goats and leading out the ones whose lust for raisins had been sated.

One goat stayed frozen at the top and ignored the treat we were offering. It wanted to turn around and retreat, so we let it. Each goat was free to choose its own best next step. But I wondered how Kovich would handle this, so I texted him. And I hinted that I'd be glad to have him at the event.

I went inside to make dinner, and as I walked away, I was amused to hear Andrea tell Frank: "Never reward a behavior that you don't want repeated."

Andrea was eager to do more training after dinner. We saw two goats spar with each other, and that helped me plan a segue into the topic of aggression.

We were well prepared when the doctors and nurses and hospital administrators arrived. Kovich showed up and ushered him to the "VIP" section. The audience seemed enthralled by the vivid depiction of how the animal brain learns. The goats also offered us a perfect demo of the animal roots of aggression. Then a Q&A led to valuable discussions of hospital procedure.

Eventually, someone asked why protesters were targeting this workshop. I said we didn't know and it was under investigation.

Another questioner expressed hostility to the method, so I introduced Doug Kovich. "He can tell you how a Harvard psychologist developed this method a century ago." I handed over the mike, and I guess Kovich was persuasive because their conversation continued into snack time.

Chi-Z flyers were proudly displayed next to the petit fours. I noticed the hostile questioner pick up a treat and carry it to the fence at Suzi's property line. There he passed it to an outstretched hand. I stared at him unashamedly, and he eventually he walked over and said, "I'm being neighborly. I saw a face there for a long time, so I decided to share. Where I grew up, you always included the neighbors in your parties." I didn't comment because he was obviously just seeking a moment of social dominance.

When everyone left, we were exhausted but thrilled. I was so grateful to Frank for devoting his vacation days to the soft launch of our soft cheese. Chi-Z wasn't ready for prime time, but we were ready to follow up with anyone interested. Frank had to go back to work the next morning, so his mind was on that. My mind drifted back to the protests. I hadn't told Frank what I'd discovered about Caterwaul because I didn't want to rock the boat before the event. I was feeling guilty about that so I decided to bring it up.

I tried to make it casual. "Until now, we've agreed not to waste energy reacting to the protests. But someone is going after us and I think we should know who and why."

"You're sounding paranoid," he said. "Maybe you're tired? I'm too busy to have enemies. I can't control these guys, so I'd rather not focus on them."

"That's logical. What if I focus on them?"

"Sure, if you think you can handle it."

I took that as a green light. So when I should have been falling asleep, I was looking for intel on Caterwaul. I had a mental image of him talking into a reporter's microphone, so I searched for that interview. It was late when I found it. I couldn't wait to hear it so I went to a room where the sound wouldn't wake anyone up.

18

Packaging

It was eerie to hear Caterwaul speak.

"I've devoted my life to helping families with the burden of ADHD. Goats cannot help these families. Goats cannot cure ADHD. My research can, and I will not let it be undermined by goat talk."

I didn't see how I was undermining his work. I didn't see how the Researcher of the Year could feel threatened by my little backyard chats on basic principles. I imagined what Frank would say, since he's had pharmaceutical clients. I imagined what Rodolfo would say, since she has families with ADHD prescriptions. I imagined what Kovich would say, since he understands PR.

Gradually, I connected the dots. I'm telling people they can learn in small steps that are rewarded, while Caterwaul is telling people they can't learn without pills.

But it still didn't add up. Why would an objective scientist go to the trouble of organizing protests against the teaching of self-management skills?

His interview sounded more like paid advertising than science. The law requires researchers to disclose potential conflicts of interest, so I searched for a disclosure. I didn't find any, and it was very late. I needed to sleep.

The next morning, I realized that Caterwaul would not disclose a conflict of interest because he'd recruited students to do the paid advocacy for him. The protests promoted the interests of his sponsors without breaking the law or jeopardizing his scientific credibility. A little searching showed me how huge the ADHD market is, which underscored the amount of money at stake.

Attention is often discussed in marketing courses, and I raised the topic in my class that day. I explained that a goat is constantly deciding where to focus its attention. When it smells a predator, its attention shifts from food to threat signals, even when it's still hungry. In the same way, we humans are always choosing where to focus our attention. You may regret a choice later on, but you are better off noticing the choices you are making. You are not better off with the belief that your attention is out of your control. Attention is not something you "have." It's something you do. You can learn to do it better just like you can learn to play the guitar better if you choose to focus on that.

I told my students that wild goats are not fed by others so they must focus their attention on foraging in order to survive. We humans have inherited a brain designed to focus on meeting survival needs. But no child is born with survival knowledge. We learn skills from early experience because behaviors that bring rewards get wired in. My students may have wondered what this had to do with marketing, but I was sure it would help their future a lot.

Maybe lack of sleep was affecting me. By the time my second lecture came, goat behavior seemed like the most important topic. Herd behavior is often discussed in marketing courses, and I knew more about it than most marketing professors. Instead of just repeating the Rousseauian view of animals, I decided to get real. I explained why animals do not stick together out of altruism. They are hiding behind each other to avoid getting eaten.

Then I explained why animals prefer to have their space. When they're too close together, they get into food fights. And they get intestinal worms because the grass underfoot has been soiled by others. Animals only cluster when they sense a threat, and then they try to save themselves by pushing toward the center of the group. A common enemy is what it takes for mammals to unite, so it's not surprising that humans talk so much about common enemies. Leaders focus on enemies because it keeps their group together.

And then it hit me. I am the enemy for Caterwaul to unite his group. He is building community by painting me as a predator and leading a fight against me.

I didn't want to be an enemy. And I didn't want to see him as an enemy. As I walked out of class, I looked for a better way to frame the problem. And it hit me. Contemporary marketing theory tells us to find our ideal customer and ignore people who don't like what we're offering. So I decided to ignore Caterwaul and focus on my ideal customer.

I explained this insight at dinner. "We can focus on people who love what we're offering instead of worrying about…others."

"How will we find the people who love it?" Andrea said.

We all sat silently for a while. Then Andrea said, "I have an idea. People seem to like learning about goats, so let's put messages about goats on the cheese package."

"I've seen cheese in little boxes," Matt said. "At school, kids take pills from little boxes that have papers folded up tiny inside. We could put our message on tiny folded paper in the box."

"Brilliant!" I said. "I'll draft the message tomorrow so we can talk about it on Saturday."

Frank said "Great! I'll design the package so we can start pitching it to distributors."

Andrea said "I'll teach the goats new tricks so we'll have more to write on the paper."

Matt said "I'll give out cheese samples at the next protest." I laughed, but then it occurred to me that he might not be joking.

After dinner, I called Rodolfo to brainstorm.

"I see a lot of those little boxes and paper inserts because my office is near the school nurse, who is legally obliged to administer any medication students take during the day. I always had a bad reaction to this, and you're helping me see why. We're giving kids the message that they should manage their brain with pills. We are not teaching them the natural way to manage their brain. Until we do, I'll be glad they can get it in the lunch room from cheese."

This was just what I needed to hear.

19

Reality Insert

I sat down to a blank screen the next morning, and after many rewrites, I figured out how to talk to people who haven't actually lived with goat. I was pleased when I came up with this:

"Welcome to the wonderful world of goats. You know that goats are mammals like us, but you may not know that a goat's brain is a lot like ours. We humans have two brains. The pink fluffy cortex you see in pictures is unique to humans, but underneath it we have the "limbic brain" that's basically the same in all mammals.

This mammal brain controls the chemicals that make us feel good and bad. Goats can't talk and your mammal brain can't tell you in words why it's releasing a good or bad feeling. This is why emotions are so hard to make sense of. Our human cortex is always trying to explain the reactions of our emotional brain. It has no insider information so it just guesses, and it's often wrong. You can make sense of your inner mammal when you know how the animal brain works.

We've been trained to think animals are effortlessly happy, but this is not true at all. Animals struggle constantly to find food, escape predators, and compete for mates. They feel great when they meet a need, and awful when they fail. But they keep striving to meet their needs because their brain releases good-feeling chemicals when they do.

A goat's brain releases a happy chemical when it sees food and a threat chemical when it smells a predator. Happy chemicals motivate a mammal to move toward rewards and threat chemicals tell it to pull back from harm. We humans feel these chemical ups and downs all the time because our brain is designed to seek rewards and avoid harm. Once our physical needs are met, social rewards spark our happy chemicals. An obstacle to social rewards triggers your threat chemicals if you're not facing a bigger threat. The chemical makes it feel like a real survival threat, even though you don't consciously think that. You can end up feeling threatened a lot, even in a very safe life.

Our verbal brain comes up with explanations for these surges of good and bad feelings. It absorbs the explanations used by those around you. It's easy to believe that your feelings are caused by external forces when you don't know how they're produced internally.

But you lose your power over your brain when you focus on externals. To find your power, let's take a closer look at how your brain manages the chemicals.

Dopamine rewards you with a great feeling when you anticipate meeting a need. Let's look at it from the perspective of our Stone Age ancestors, since their survival needs were more obvious. Imagine you're thirsty and you see an oasis in the distance. Your dopamine surges, which makes you feel good while you step toward it. Imagine you're cold and you go out in the snow to find firewood. Now you're even colder, but the good

Loretta Breuning

feeling of dopamine turns on as soon as you see a way to meet a need. Our ancestors survived because dopamine rewarded them for taking action.

Dopamine stops once your reach the oasis or make the fire. Our brain is not designed to give you dopamine all the time. It couldn't do its job of motivating you if it did. Dopamine turns off once the need is met, and you have to meet another need to get more. You may not like this idea, but you are better off knowing the truth.

In today's world, physical needs are met more easily, so we look to social needs to spark our happy chemicals. Oxytocin is the good feeling that it's safe to let down your guard. A goat lets down its guard when it sees other goats. When it's alone, it's so busy scanning for predators that it can hardly eat. When others are around, they share the burden of vigilance so a goat can relax. Oxytocin creates that good feeling. Humans look for social support because oxytocin makes it feel good.

We want oxytocin all the time, but it could not do its job if it were always on. You would let down your guard when it wasn't really safe. Our brain evolved to make good decisions about when to release it. A mammal is always looking for safe opportunities to lower its guard.

We've been trained to romanticize animals, so we think they have cozy supportive groups all the time. But the animal urge for protection is quite selfish. Animals push toward the center of the herd to protect themselves from predators. They prefer to forage alone to avoid food fights and contamination. But a lone mammal is vulnerable to predators, so their brain is *always weighing the costs of benefits of sticking with the group. We humans do the same. Following the crowd has a cost, but oxytocin is the benefit.*

Serotonin complicates the social lives of mammals a lot more. It creates the good feeling of self-confidence. We would like to have this feeling all the time, but the mammal brain saves the serotonin for moments when it sees itself in a position of strength. A goat stays out of the way of stronger goats to protect itself from harm. If its serotonin were always on, it would get into fight that it would lose. The mammal brain is designed to save serotonin for those moments when it sees that it can win.

You may not want to believe this about animals or humans, but life makes sense when you know the facts about our neurochemical operating system. Serotonin feels so good that we long to be the bigger goat all the time. But if you expect to have this feeling all the time, you will be disappointed. Realistic expectations help you enjoy life.

In the animal world, stronger group-mates take food and mates from weaker group-mates. A mammal looks for a position of strength in order to relieve its hunger. This may seem harsh. We'd rather believe that animals cooperate and share, but we benefit from knowing the facts. That doesn't mean we should bully weaker individuals. It means we should know why our brain makes social comparisons and has life-or-death feelings about them. Then we can stop taking these feelings so seriously.

The mammal brain rewards you with serotonin when you find a way to get ahead. Whether you're in a cooking contest or a video game or an argument, you want to win because serotonin makes it feel good. Tiny steps toward a win spark tiny drips of serotonin, which motivates you to take more steps. This is why people keep looking for opportunities to be in the one-up position and fearing the one-down position.

This is not what you've heard about serotonin. No one likes these facts because they conflict with the Rousseauian beliefs embedded in our education system. But you can see for yourself that people care about social dominance, and you can it in animals if you read books written before the warm-fuzzy era. (Here's a list: InnerMammalInstitute.org/readinglist.)

Pets do not give us a realistic view of animals. Pets do not have to find their own food or compete for mates. They do not use their brains for the job it was naturally selected for. We need to understand wild animals to understand our own chemistry. When people lived alongside wild animals, they knew the truth. They would have laughed at you if you said that animals are altruistic and empathetic. Today's false view of animals makes it hard to understand our own animal brain.

It's hard to accept our mammalian feelings because our culture says we shouldn't think this way. But if you don't see how you create these feelings inside you, you will believe they are forced on you by external forces. You will end up feeling like a powerless victim. Instead, you can build a sense of strength without being a bully.

Bad-feeling chemicals help a mammal survive as much as happy chemicals. Cortisol is the chemical that tells a mammal that its life is in danger. A goat seeks greener pastures because dopamine makes it feel good, but cortisol tells it when it has gone too far. A goat asserts itself to get food or a mate, but cortisol tells it when it's likely to lose. When your cortisol turns on, you feel like you're going to die, even if it was just triggered by a small social disappointment.

To understand these emotions, we need to know about the old neural pathways that guide them. The chemicals of emotion are like paving on your neural pathways. They wire you to feel good when you see something that felt good before and feel bad about things that felt bad before. No conscious logic is involved, so these links may not make logical sense. They're just your brain's way of helping you act fast when you see an opportunity or a threat. Each brain defines good and bad based on its own past experience.

We rely on old neural pathways without knowing it because the electricity in the brain flows like water in a storm, finding the paths of least resistance. We flow into grooves that are already there the way a car drives on roads that are already paved. You flow into old pathways so easily that you don't realize you have a choice. You have billions of extra neurons ready to see the world in new ways. You don't use them because it's so hard to get electricity to flow into them. It's like trying to get a river to flow into a soda straw. This is why we all tend to repeat ourselves, getting excited about whatever met our needs before and fearing whatever threatened us before.

Fortunately, we have the power to pump the brakes and redirect our electricity. But it's hard. It's a skill you learn with practice like any other skill. Your quality of life depends on this skill, so it's worth practicing.

It's hard to see mammalian impulses in yourself and your friends. It's easier to see them in people you don't like. When you and your friends do crazy things for dopamine, it feels like you have a good reason. But when people outside your circle do crazy things for dopamine, the problem seems obvious.

When someone you don't like tries to gain the one-up position, you may call it manipulation and ego. But when someone you like seeks the one-up position, you may call it dignity and pride. Our verbal brain is always trying to make us look good, which gets in the way of understanding our real chemistry. This is why the animal perspective is so useful.

Whenever a goat sees another goat, it decides whether it is in the position or strength or the position of weakness. They communicate this to the other goat with body language that all goats recognize. Goats only fight when both individuals perceive themselves as the likely winner. The mammal brain is good at weighing its strength, so fights are usually avoided. But the mammal brain is busy making social comparisons a lot, which is why you will flow into this thought loop a lot if you don't practice redirecting.

Neurons connect when serotonin flows, which wires you to seek the position of strength in ways that worked for you before. You don't like to think of yourself as someone who seeks social dominance, so your verbal brain finds a socially acceptable way to explain that urge. You tell yourself that you are serving the greater good.

When you fail to get the one-up moment you seek, cortisol can make it feel like a survival threat. And when you succeed, the serotonin doesn't last. The chemicals is quickly metabolized, which is why mammals are always looking for more. This is why people are often sparring for position of one sort or another. It's taboo to express this urge in most cultures, so we're tempted to ignore it in ourselves and demonize it in our rivals.

You may think other people float through life on an endless cloud of serotonin and you are missing out. But no one has it all the time because that would lead to unnecessary conflicts. Don't think the alpha goat has a better life because it is constantly challenged by beta goats who want its position. Our happy chemicals are only meant to turn on in short spurts when the moment is right.

You have been taught that happiness is the default state of nature and unhappiness is evidence that something has gone wrong. You may think you can't be happy until something is fixed. You are better off knowing the truth. Nothing is wrong. We are all mammals. Our brain saves the happy chemicals to motivate survival action. We want them all the time but they are not designed to be on all the time. We seek them all the time, but our efforts will not always succeed. This is the challenge that comes with the gift of life.

20

Connecting Dots

On Saturday morning, Frank and the kids sat down to scrutinize my manifesto.

"It's soooo long, Mom," Andrea said.

"I can cut it," Matt said.

I was not happy. Every word was essential to me. We debated and came up with a good compromise. They would cut it into chunks and print each with a different goat image. "Collect all of them" is a meme that comes easily to their generation. From a marketing perspective, it made sense.

But I still felt that the whole had value, so we agreed to put it all on one sheet in small print on special occasions. Buck and Bunnie's birthdays were the first occasions we agreed on. The kids wanted to celebrate the birthdays of goats who became popular. I had trouble imagining celebrity goats, so we agreed to decide this if and when it happened.

As the Chi-Z meeting wound down, Doug Kovich called. Some nurses he met at our event asked him to host a workshop so they could learn more about aggression and reward-learning in animals. He didn't think his zoo would approve, so he invited them to discuss it in person while viewing the animals.

"I told them that our zoo is a large bureaucracy with all the caution and competition of any herd of mammals. Even if the zoo agreed to host an event, I knew they'd only focus on the kindness of animals. And I figure the nurses already that from Human Resources."

"They must have been disappointed," I replied.

"Not exactly," he said. "They pressured me to fight the zoo administrators, and even tried to shame me into it, saying "aren't your horns big enough?' Why would they do that to me? I was just trying to help them without losing my job."

"I suspect they were teasing you, Doug. I even suspect that they like you."

"I guess I'm being hypersensitive. You can guess why, I'm sure."

"Because of the size of your horns?"

"No!" He sputtered and then realized I was kidding. "I'm worried about protestors showing up here at the zoo. I'd get fired if that happened. Who wants a marketing director who attracts protests?"

"Why would protestors show up at the zoo?"

"Why do they show up anywhere? We don't know, do we?"

I didn't want to tell him what I knew because it was not solid yet. I wanted to say no one would protest a zoo, but my all predictions had been wrong so far. So I blandly reassured him that I'd get to the bottom of it. I felt guilty for failing to give him the protection from a common enemy that he was hoping for. But I was focused on our upcoming cheese launch. My mammal was doing its job of choosing where to allocate my limited energy. Like a goat deciding when it's worth climbing a steep hill for fresh grass, and when it's worth sticking with the herd. Goats don't second-guess their decisions because they don't have enough neurons. The human brain is big enough to over-analyze everything, so I decided to be like a goat and move on.

Part 2

Two Years Later

1

Spreading Wings

Chi-Z orders rolled in!

Maybe it was Frank's beautiful packaging. Maybe it was Bunnie's expert processing. Maybe it was Andrea's fabulous recipes. And maybe my insert contributed something.

At first, we only had a trickle of orders. But mothers were slipping those inserts into their family's lunches, so our product got noticed by teachers and coworkers. People started eating goat cheese and jelly sandwiches instead of PB&J, and some even claimed they switched to get more inserts. People passed them around and the buzz boosted sales. Things got so busy that I took a leave of absence from my university and stopped offering backyard seminars on the mammal brain.

We didn't do much marketing because we wanted to get the product right first. And we didn't chase media attention because of the bad experience with protests. But now, Frank thought he thought he could really make something happen if he worked at it full time. So he quit his day job too, and we were suddenly like trapeze artists without a net.

But the future looked bright. Marketing theory tells us to focus on market share rather than profitability. It presumes that profit will come once you capture a good chunk of a market. Chi-Z had captured a nice share of the goat-cheese market, and it even managed to increase goat cheese as a share of the total cheese market.

The golden fleece of the marketing world is to create a new market that never existed before. Then you have it all to yourself. We did that twice! We built a lunch market as well as a dessert market for goat cheese. This was such an accomplishment that other cheese companies took notice.

One of them was owned by a huge global conglomerate, and they wanted to buy us out.

We did not see this as an attack. We had never intended to devote our lives to cheese. We were exhausted by years of working around the clock, and we'd reached the limit of our skill set. We also reached the limit of our production capacity, so we knew we'd need a partner. We were happy to sell because we'd met our original goal of keeping the farm and using our skills to create something.

But there was one condition: the insert had to stay. Our lawyers put that into the contract, and we made sure to find lawyers who knew how to do this. The investors resisted at first and presumed we'd cave. They had never seen acquisition terms tied to an "insert." But when they paused the deal, we got two more offers for the company. So the big conglomerate raised its bid and agreed to our terms.

While the lawyers were filing the documents, we started planning a well-deserved vacation.

Matt wanted us to take our vacation to a place with wild goats. He'd been interested in them since his Biology teacher explained the difference between wild animals and domesticated. Now he was writing his senior thesis on wild goats and begged us for a chance to observe them. Andrea chimed in that they're "sooooo cute" and she "had to" see them.

Frank and I agreed that it's a great goal for the future, but we need R&R right now. I added that wild animals hide, so our chances of actually seeing them were low. Real life never looks like a video because videographers hide for weeks in tiny lookouts with long-distance lenses.

The slow unwinding of the legal process gave me time to think about my future. I was still on leave from teaching and wasn't sure if I wanted to go back. As I wrestled with the thought, I decided to stroll through campus. My feet somehow led to the Teacher Education building instead of the Marketing Department. Perhaps the cheese deal had raised my confidence, because I found myself walking up the stairs to the Department of Educational Neuroscience and turning into Caterwaul's corridor.

The "Caterwaul Lab" sign leapt out at me. It was eerie to see something I had imagined so often but never actually looked at. A lot of students were going in and out, and some stood chatting in the hallway. I noticed a lot of movement near a different door, so I walked over and saw that it was a break room with vending machines.

I walked up to the vending machines and took my time examining their wares. I overheard lots of chatter but it was hard to make out anything. I bought some juice and took a seat. Then I struggled to decipher the chatter while pretending to read.

I couldn't pick up whole sentences, but I kept hearing the words "brain pill." I searched on those words, and soon found an actual product called "BrainPill." A press release said that after years of rigorous research, BrainPill would soon revolutionize human knowledge. It was made by a company called Blue Water Laboratories. I couldn't find much about them except that they're headquartered on St. Kitts in the Caribbean.

Suddenly, St. Kitts seemed like the perfect vacation choice. I went home and proposed it, and everyone agreed. I felt guilty for not revealing my ulterior motive, but I rationalized that the island's beautiful blue water should stand on its own merits.

2

Blue Waters

I booked the trip for the day after we signed the papers and handed off the company. Frank took a job in their Marketing Department, and I agreed to consult on operations as needed for one year. But it was agreed that our vacation came first.

I reserved a suite in a beautiful resort on the ocean, which just happened to be across the street from Blue Water Laboratories. I was gratified to see their discreet sign as our taxi turned into our lavishly landscaped hotel.

The kids were eager to go to the beach as soon as we put down our luggage. Frank went with them, but I said I wanted to explore the resort facilities. Now I had an actual lie to feel guilty about, but I promised myself that I'd confess everything at dinner. First, I couldn't wait to stroll past the lab.

There wasn't a lot to see because all the blinds were closed. I could see a receptionist by peeking through the door. I couldn't figure out how to penetrate this fortress and I thought Frank would be good at it, so I went back to the beach. Soon I was describing the vending machines, the juice, and the pill that would revolutionize human knowledge.

"What the heck is BrainPill!?" Frank erupted.

"That's exactly what I was thinking. Don't you want to find out? What if the answer was a five-minute stroll from where we are now?"

They all looked at me suspiciously. Instead of answering in words, I started walking and they followed. In five minutes, we stood in front of the Blue Water sign and I casually mentioned that BrainPill was produced there. They were too shocked to say anything. Frank looked annoyed and I hoped it was the idea of the pill rather than my intrigue. We agreed to sleep on it.

In the morning, Frank announced that the kids were old enough to go to the beach without us. But they figured out what we were up to and insisted on joining our spy mission rather than going to the beach. So we all marched through the lobby of the hotel and down the lavishly landscaped driveway to the office park across the street. Frank walked in and the receptionist asked if he had an appointment. He couldn't think of a good answer, so he said he had mistaken this for his dentist's office.

We snooped around outside, but nothing looked significant. We passed a little cafe and Matt suggested we have lunch there. So we went to the beach and then tramped back down the driveway at lunchtime. It was fun to eat in a place full of local food and local people, but we didn't pick up any leads. I may have watched too many detective shows because I peered into trash containers on the way back to the hotel. I was starting to feel guilty for leading the family down a blind alley.

As we tramped through the lobby again, the desk clerk said, "I know what you're up to." We all froze. I tried not to look guilty.

"We don't get many guests walking over to the industrial park, so when we see it, we know why." We must have looked as uncomfortable as we felt because he followed up with, "Don't worry, I won't tell anyone."

"So you know?" Frank said, with his usual calm.

"Good luck. I hope you get the job. Don't worry, I won't tell anyone there's an opening."

We all exhaled.

"It's a good company," the desk clerk continued. "They're doing big things."

I wanted to ask what big things, but a real job applicant would know that. So I paused to think of something better.

Frank had an idea. "It's a huge decision to uproot the family, but I guess they're worth it."

"We have a great school for the kids. All the ex-pats go to St. Kitts Academy. My cousin runs it. He would love to meet you. I'll call him." He picked up the phone and tapped a button as he said this.

I was afraid to be rude, so I said, "Thanks, that would be nice."

Loretta Breuning

As the phone rang, he said, "To tell you the truth, Mr. Symonds loves to meet parents here because we pay for the dinner. Our cousin owns this hotel. Are you free for dinner tonight?"

"That sounds good," Frank said. "Do you have a cousin at Blue Water?"

"Of course," he said. "We're all cousins on this island. Don't worry. I already put in a good word for you."

"How kind of you," he said. I nervously looked around and saw that the walls were covered with the framed photos of the Symonds cousins shaking hands with local dignitaries. One showed them with the CEO of Blue Water! I was thrilled to have plugged into this network.

"He'll meet you at seven o'clock in the restaurant," the desk clerk said.

3

World Premiere

Before dinner, we played ping pong in the hotel rec room. An older local man walked over and challenged Matt and Andrea to play him two-against-one. While they played, Frank and I checked our messages to make sure the Chi-Z hand-off was on track. When seven o'clock came and Mr. Symonds didn't appear, I realized that the pingpong challenger was Mr. Symonds.

I whispered to Frank and we put down our phones. When a game ended, we applauded and introduced ourselves. Then we sat down with the elite of St. Kitts. He said to call him Sy because that's how everyone on the island knows him.

"Thank you for your interest in St. Kitts Academy." That made me squirm, but before I had a chance to sweat, he offered music to my ears. "We are proud to have the world's premier program for the treatment of Knowledge Resistance Disorder. My cousin invented BrainPill, so your lovely children will be able to access it long before the rest of the world."

Frank and I stared at each other. "Congratulations to your cousin," I said.

"I wish I knew more about Knowledge Resistance Disorder," Frank said.

Sy was glad to elaborate. "I spend a lot of my time talking to families who have tried everything, and they're thrilled to hear the amazing results we've had with BrainPill."

"Nice," Frank said.

"Many of our students were treated for ADHD, or prescribed with SSRI, or medicated for bipolar disorder. But nothing worked because the underlying Knowledge Resistance Disorder wasn't treated. That's where we come in." He smiled as if he were expecting the Nobel Peace Prize.

"It sounds like you provide a very valuable service," I said.

"Indeed. I hear that from so many families."

"So how do you treat them exactly?" Frank asked.

"We have exclusive access to the outstanding research of Blue Water Laboratories." The kids inhaled when those words were spoken. "Blue Water developed the world's premiere treatment for KRD. And they keep fine-tuning it with the world's top experts. Each refinement of the formula goes to our students immediately. So you see there is nothing better you can do for your children than to enroll them in our program. If you enroll now, they will still have a four-month lead before the worldwide commercial launch.

"So it launches in four months?" Frank said. "And I still don't really know what KRD is. Can you please say more about it?" I was relieved that Frank spoke up because I would have unleashed a torrent of sarcasm if I said anything.

"Our patented formula is a non-narcotic, non-methylic, plant-based cognitive enhancer."

I almost burst out laughing and strained to hold it in.

Sy turned to the kids. "Matt and Andrea, imagine being able to sit down and absorb your preferred course of study with delight."

"Sure," Andrea said. I was glad for the kids to absorb the slack. I trusted them to see through his snake oil.

"Sure," said Matt. "But I don't have Knowledge Resistance Disorder."

"Our research shows that a huge percentage of cases have not been diagnosed. We are teaching young people to recognize the symptoms. It can have serious consequences if not treated in time, so you are lucky to have landed here! Your friends won't be able to get their hands on BrainPill for four months, so you are fortunate indeed."

Enough. I couldn't wait for this meal to be over. I contemplated moving to a new hotel, or even booking an earlier departure just to distance myself from this slime. But the kids made me proud.

"I don't understand what the pill does," said Andrea, with youthful directness.

"It stimulates new neural synapses when taken as part of a complete mental-health diet," Sy answered. Matt and Andrea looked at each other and smiled. Then they looked at Sy and nodded.

"What is a complete mental-health diet?" Matt asked.

"Healthy food, exercise, sleep hygiene, and rewards for academic excellence." I unclench my fists a little when I heard this. It sounded like a fancy placebo, luring people to do the right thing with a high price tag. That was annoying, but not as bad as a drug that interfered with natural functions.

"We'll think seriously about St. Kitts Academy," I said. Dinner was almost over but I couldn't resist one more question. "What exactly is happening in four months?"

"If I knew I couldn't tell you, but the truth is that I don't know. Blue Water Labs has been working on BrainPill for a long time, and they will not release it until it is perfect. Patents are pending in major markets so we're also waiting until they're issued."

Sy offered dessert and we said we had no room. He said our meal was on the house, and we thanked him with grave sincerity while walking backwards out of the room. I sighed deeply as the door closed.

"I still don't understand what Knowledge Resistance Disorder is," Andrea said.

"It's fake!" Matt said, "Don't you get it? They're selling a fake cure for a fake disease."

Matt looked at us, knowing that we object when he uses that condescending tone on his sister. But we were ecstatic that he said out loud what we were thinking. Our approval pleased him, so he actually apologized to his sister.

I had trouble sleeping that night. A piece of the puzzle was still missing: Blue Water's link to Caterwaul. I was dying to ask that, but afraid of sounding like a spy. Sy probably had a cousin on the police force.

Frank couldn't sleep either. "There's still a big unanswered question," Frank said. But his question was different. "If it's just a fancy nutritional supplement, how did it get so much research funding?"

"Maybe they're laundering drug money," I said.

"Maybe there is no research."

"So how are they bankrolling Caterwaul? And why?"

We finally fell asleep without answers.

4

Dolphin Wars

St. Kitts has a dolphinarium in its little capital city, so we decided to spend our last vacation day swimming with these amazing marine mammals.

We had to wait our turn on a long line. To pass the time, I asked the kids if they'd like to enroll at St Kitts Academy. I was just being facetious, but Andrea surprised me by saying "yeaaaaah." She seemed to see it as an endless beach party.

"Yuck," Matt said. "They'd force you to take brain pills."

We watched dolphins swimming around in a pool next to the ticket line. Andrea noticed scratches and scarring all over them. Once we got in, she asked their trainer about it and he said, "They scrape each other with their teeth all the time. Don't worry. It heals fast. Then they do it again."

We smiled at each other, recognizing the familiar pattern of goats. And of mammals! Matt started searching on dolphin aggression, but it was our turn to swim.

We enjoyed it tremendously. The kids knew how to be gentle with the dolphins after all their time in the goatyard. It was amazing to see the scratches and scars up close. The half hour went by too quickly.

Matt went back to researching dolphin aggression as soon as he got his clothes back on. He found the trainer to ask questions.

"It's just play," the trainer said.

"Shiiiiit!" Matt shouted, and ran outside to the street.

We ran after him. He was still saying "shitshitshit" when we caught up. He had never acted like this before. I stared at him waiting for an answer.

"Why do people lie?" he said.

"What's going on with you?" Frank asked.

"Why do they say 'it's just play'? It's not just play. It's painful. It's serious."

"True, but why are you so upset about this?" I presumed he was being bullied at school, as any mother would think. But it was something different.

"I wrote an essay on goat aggression in my psychology class. The teacher gave me a bad grade and wrote 'it's just play' in red letters at the top. She accused me of not doing my research! It can't believe how unfair that it."

"I'm glad you told us. It is unfair. I would love to tell that teacher…" That was the wrong thing to say. Matt would be humiliated if his mother did his fighting for him.

In the taxi on the way back to the hotel, Frank said "Can I tell you about 'cognitive dissonance'?"

Andrea rolled her eyes as she felt a lecture coming, but I was glad he raised the topic.

"When facts conflict with a person's beliefs, they don't change their beliefs. They denigrate the facts. People have always done this and always will, so it doesn't pay to take it personally."

"How can a teacher be so stupid?" Matt spat out.

"No one wants to see flaws in their explanatory framework. Her friends and co-workers probably share her explanatory framework, so she'd risk these relationships if she accepted your facts. It's easier to insult the facts and insult the person who reported them."

"What's an explanatory framework?" Andrea said.

"We all have beliefs that help us make sense of the world," Frank said. "Teachers typically believe that nature is good and everything bad comes from society. So if they accepted the natural aggression of the mammal brain, that would lead to conclusions that scare them."

"Why would they be scared?" Andrea followed up.

"Because we'd all have to learn to manage our aggression instead of blaming it on a theoretical abstraction called 'society.'"

"Why would that be scary?" Matt asked.

"Mammal groups often bond around a common enemy. Humans often do that by making society the enemy. So you're out of the group if you stop blaming society. The mammal brain equates social isolation with being eaten by a predator, and that's why it's scary."

"The human brain has a funny way of deciding what's true," I went on. "Our neurons are not connected when we're born. We connect them from early experience, so we all see the world through the lens of our own past. We 're not aware of our wiring, so we think we're just seeing the facts. But the electricity in the brain flows into pathways that are already developed and has trouble flowing into unfamiliar territory. So new information often seems wrong, and we don't know how we've spun it with our old neural pathways.

We arrived at the hotel and the kids went to shower, so I rushed to speak privately to Frank.

"I think there's more to this than just a bad grade. Maybe Matt got his heart broken when a girl chose a guy with bigger horns."

"Of course. I should have thought of that. Social rivalry is so painful for young males."

"And they don't know where the pain comes from. Even adults don't understand the mammal brain's sense of urgency about reproductive success. It feels like a real emergency. Maybe you talk to him about it?"

"I will. I can even take him for a beer in this country. The small size glass. We'll go now and meet you in the dining room after."

While I was alone with Andrea, I asked her why she wanted to go to St. Kitts Academy. "The girls at my school are mean. They fight and I don't like to hear it. But after the dolphins, I think I get it. The girls in St. Kitts would probably have drama too."

"Exactly. You can choose your response to it, but you can't choose how people are because they will always be mammals."

When we gathered for dinner, Frank had a good way to frame the topic: "It's hard to live with the reality of mammals competing for social dominance, but when you know that it's natural, it's easier to relax about it."

"You mean we shouldn't care about who is dominating us?" Matt said.

"Not at all," I said. "I mean we shouldn't believe we are dominated just because of one incident."

"Imagine I have ten different paths in front of me," Frank said. If that unfair teacher is blocking one path, I can choose to focus on the others."

"I get it!" Matt said, and he looked genuinely happy.

"I don't get it," Andrea said. "A girl in my class is always telling me she got a better grade on a test, and I get upset. Are you saying she was born smarter and I should forget about it?"

"No, that's not at all what I'm saying. We don't know her whole story. Your mammal brain wants to focus on social comparison, but you don't really benefit from that. Focus on what you have control over, like studying."

"Let's look at it from a goat's perspective," Frank said. "Imagine I pull out two goats for training. After I finish with the first one, it can do something that the second goat can't do. Does the second goat think it's stupid?"

"OK, I get it," Andrea said.

"Goats are not born knowing how to find food," I added. They learn from following their mother. If they don't learn, they go hungry. They enjoy a full belly when they imitate their mother. Hunger was the motivator for all of our ancestors. Modern humans are challenged to learn without the threat of hunger."

"Modern humans don't want to learn from their mothers either," Frank added.

"I have a question," Matt said. If a goat spends its whole life finding food the way it learned when it was young, and my teacher spends her whole life believing whatever she learned when she was young, does anyone ever change?"

"It goes back to hunger," I said. "Let's say a goat loses access to familiar foods. They refuse new foods until they're very hungry. Then they try a little, and if they end up feeling better, they have more. The brain learns from any behavior that shifts a bad feeling to a good feeling."

"If a goat gets an extra-large meal from a particular plant, the good feeling will wire it to look for that plant,"

Frank said. "Extra-large rewards build extra-large pathways in the brain."

"His teacher might learn something new if she's hungry or if she gets and extra-large reward," Andrea said. "But he should focus on his path rather than his teacher's path."

We all applauded Andrea's excellent summary. Then Matt said, "Now I know what to do!" But he wouldn't tell us.

5

Knowledge Resistance

Waiting at the airport for our flight home, I couldn't wait to catch up with Rodolfo. I sent her a text about Sy's "Knowledge Resistance Disorder" and was glad to see her response when we landed. But it was not what I expected.

"He read my mind," she said. "When I was a classroom teacher, it often seemed like students were actively resisting knowledge."

I wrote back while waiting at Baggage Claim, "But why call it a disorder?"

"I took that in a tongue-in-cheek way."

"But they're serious," I replied. "The word give them license to give out pills instead of teaching kids to manage their brain. That just leads to more pills."

"True. I guess I'm just so eager for a solution. Do you have a better one?"

"What we've been saying all along! The brain learns from rewards."

"Hasn't that been tried?"

"Not really, because kids get rewarded for not learning as much as they get rewarded for learning."

No reply. Did I offend her? I worried about it in my sudden abundance of free time. So I called her.

"Let's talk in person because the issue is too big for writing," she said. "And in truth, I'm afraid to put some things into writing."

So she came to the goatyard after work, and I pounced on her after pouring tea: "What are you afraid to put into writing?"

She took a deep breath. "Teachers are pressured to pass students who don't do passing work. We say 'they'll catch up,' but often they don't. They give up because the gap between their skills and their coursework is too big. And we keep passing them, so a student could graduate high school with a third grade reading level. Wheeew. I said it."

"Wow. It's like asking a goat to leap across a gap that's too big for its body. Rewards only work when the goal is broken down into steps that are doable for that individual."

"Teachers can't do that in today's system. We'd be condemned if we gave simpler work to a student with simpler skills. We're also condemned for giving rewards."

"So what can a teacher do with a disengaged student?"

"We find ways to give them points that don't require academic skills. Students figure out that points are what matters and learn ways to get points without actually building skills. We call this 'compensatory' skills. It includes everything from being cute to being nasty to good old-fashioned cheating."

"Imagine how scary it is for a kid to spend every day surrounded by tasks they can't decode."

"Exactly. It's humiliating, so students learn cover it up. They get very good at deflecting attention when they're on the spot."

"I imagine it's scary for teachers too – standing in front of students who learned to game the system but didn't learn basic skills. I've had this feeling in my college classes. I've seen students work harder at diversionary measures than it would have taken to just do the coursework. So it occurred to me that doing the work doesn't feel like an option for them."

"It's sad that these kids are pressured to go to college. We don't offer an alternative, so a kid expects their compensatory skills to keep working for them."

"If they landed in jail, people would worry, but if they land in college, it's counted as a success. Colleges pretend that remedial courses can fix these huge skill deficits in a few months. The truth becomes unmentionable."

"It all boils down to the reward structure imposed on teachers. They get blamed if they fail a student, but if they pass a student who lacks competence, they're safe."

"The reward structure for students is a problem too. Help is available, but if a student refuses help, there are no consequences."

"Or if they resist help, to use Sy's word."

I started to laugh, but I saw how serious she was.

"The word resonated with me because resistance is a real physical thing. Once a child panics in response to a learning task, they avoid learning in order to avoid panic."

"That could be re-trained the way we retrain a goat who panics at the vet."

"But that solution is not in fashion this year. Pills are in fashion. So now what?"

"I'm still thinking about it."

6

Smashing Skulls

On our first day back home, Matt asked when we could go see wild goats. "We just had a vacation!" I said.

"This isn't vacation. It's research."

I jumped to the conclusion that he wanted to avoid school, but he had a nice surprise.

"I signed up for the debate team, and I proposed a debate on animal aggression. I don't want to be accused of not doing my research so I want to trek after wild goats."

"Debate is a great idea," Frank said. "You'll get to express yourself without that teacher as a gatekeeper. But the debate team can't expect you to do empirical research."

"But let's keep it as a future goal," I said.

"Yes, I would love to see wild goats someday," Frank said.

"Me too!" said Andrea.

I told them all about my conversation with Rodolfo. It was a heavy subject for kids, but I wanted their observations since they're first-hand witnesses to the situation.

"I know what you mean," Andrea said. "A kid in my class cries when she's called on, so the teacher doesn't call on her. Another kid gets angry when it's his turn to contribute in his group, so stopped expecting him to contribute."

Matt had a different example. "Last month, a teacher asked me to help a kid study. I tried and tried, but he didn't take in anything I said. Afterwards, he told the teacher that I teased him, but I swear I didn't. I think he felt bad and just blamed it on me."

"I can see why Blue Water chose to focus on knowledge resistance," Frank said. "But their solution reminds me of the Wizard of Oz, where the Scarecrow feels smart because the Wizard gave him a diploma. Now, a pill does the job."

Matt went to his room to start preparing for his debate. I heard a loud noise, so I knocked on the door. It was just background music on a video of two mountain goats fighting. Matt welcomed me to watch it with him. Soon, Frank and Andrea were watching too.

One goat stood up on its hind legs and crashed its skull into the rival's skull with its full body weight. Then the other goat did the same. They did this over and over and over. I couldn't imagine such stamina.

"They're very motivated because the winner gets all the females and there's only one mating season a year," Matt said. "So if a guy never wins, his genes are annihilated from the face of the earth. Today's wild goats are descended from the biggest skull smashers."

"That's a good explanation," I told him. "I hope you're using it in the debate. When is it?"

"Next week," he said.

"I can see that you'll be well prepared."

"I haven't figured out how to fit it all into five minutes."

"You might write up everything you now and then pare it down. You will surely find a use for the full version later on."

Andrea joined in the spirit of things. "Mom, I want to do more training with the goats tomorrow after school."

"That sounds great. I'll give Buck a heads up."

The next day, I watched Andrea's training session from a distance so she would feel in charge. Her second trainee froze at the top of the seesaw and wouldn't budge. "Can't I just give him one raisin to cheer him up?" she said to Buck "The poor little guy looks so scared."

That put Buck in a bad position. He knew it was wrong to reward a goat who refuses to take the desired step, but he didn't want to discourage Andrea. He looked at me, hoping I would be the bad guy. Of course, I was hoping he would be the heavy. This is exactly what Rodolfo was talking about. It's uncomfortable for a teacher to hold the line so everyone hopes someone else will do it.

I said nothing. Buck said nothing. Andrea said "She must be hungry," Andrea said. "A raisin will give her the energy to move."

Then I had an idea. If she does it, she will learn that it doesn't work. I whispered that into in Buck's ear, and he told Andrea "Fine, try it."

Andrea fed the frozen goat, but it stayed glued to the spot. It stared at her relentlessly, so she gave it more raisins, not even consulting us this time. The goat just kept staring at her. Finally, it turned around and walked back down the seesaw. Then it nudged her leg. The goat had learned that getting Andrea's attention is the path to rewards. It did not learn to get a reward by mastering its fear of moving forward.

Andrea looked like she was about to cry. Then she burst out, "I get it! You knew it wouldn't work! You told Buck to let me do it so I'd see that it doesn't work." That moment is burned into my memory. It was one of those painful parenting moments when your kid learns a harsh reality. Andrea learned that rewarding bad behavior brings more bad behavior, even if you do it with good intentions. It's easier to learn this with goats, since with humans, the bad consequences are not so immediate. And humans can always find someone else who will give them a raisin if they nudge enough.

Andrea didn't give up. The next day after school, she went out to train more goats. When one of them froze in terror, she put the raisin closer to its foot. She would not let go of that reward until the goat moved forward an inch. And it did! Then she worked on the next inch. Soon, the goat was moving with ease.

7

Roadblock

Matt won the debate! Now he would go on to represent his school at a regional debate. We were so proud.

But the next week, the Principal called him in to say that he could not debate on animal aggression. "Just pick another topic," she said. He asked why and she wouldn't say. Matt got upset, and the Principal said it was not her decision.

I got mad when I heard this. I wanted to do something but Matt begged me to stay out of it. So I waited until he left for school the next morning and then called the Principal. She said "I was expecting to hear from you…Our school cannot appear to condone violence."

I told her that explaining animal behavior does not condone violence in humans. "On the contrary, it helps prevent violence by showing that self-restraint must be learned. How can kids learn this essential skill if we can't talk about it?"

"Studies show that animals cooperate," the Principal said. "We learn that in teacher training, and that's what we teach our students. You can't change the facts just because you own goats."

"With all due respect," I said, though I was not feeling much respect, "you can't change reality just because professors construct studies that tell people what they want to hear."

"I didn't design the Teacher Education curriculum. I'm just doing… what's expected of me."

I could see the tightrope she was on. She wanted to keep her job, but didn't want to say she agreed with the warm-fuzzy cult. Good. I was in her shoes before I became a cheese mogul, so I decided to share. "I worked inside the sausage factory, so I know how these so-called studies are made. Results that support shared beliefs bring grant money and promotions and public recognition. Results that conflict with shared beliefs bring ridicule and attack."

"I have another meeting," she said. I was glad to hear that since I had no more to say and didn't need to hear a rebuttal.

I smiled and got up to leave, and then realized that I did have more to say. "Invoking the greater good can help you win an argument but that doesn't mean the greater good is actually served."

"I can see where your son gets his debate skills. You've made some good points. This was not my decision."

In the end, I did respect her. She helped us as much as she could without losing her job. She said it was not her decision to Matt and to me, so where did the decision come from? I called Rodolfo.

She looked into it and reported back. "The gossip is that the debate teacher complained to the Superintendent, saying it felt like a threat of violence. The Superintendent caved and called the High School Principal. So I got us a meeting with the Superintendent tomorrow."

He greeted us with a fake smile. "Let's be direct," he said. "Your son told the audience that female goats accept whichever male wins the fight. Mrs. Jaynes, how can we support such an unhealthy message? Do you think our young ladies need to hear that?"

"It's basic biology," I said. "Students must understand their biology in order to manage it."

"I was told that students left your son's speech thinking it's cool to fight."

"So you want to cancel biological facts because of this hearsay opinion?"

Rodolfo scribbled a note and passed it to me: "I don't think you're helping your son anymore." But I thought I was helping, so I continued.

"My son told them: 'You're not a goat. You have better ways to compete for attention. But we need to know that we all have this mammalian urge to compete for attention.' I think that message benefited plenty of students."

"I guess I'll have to delve into this," he said, hanging his head.

"I can help you delve into it if you'd like," I said, but Rodolfo had already pulled my sleeve out the door, so he may not have heard.

8

Disillusionment

"Moooom, what did you say to the Principal?"

"A lot. Do you want to hear it all?"

"My debate coach cancelled me from the regionals. I asked her why and she said 'These things happen.' It's so unfair."

I was furious. I wanted to scream or cry, but I also wanted to set a good example for my son. I told him that he shouldn't take it personally because the problem is deeper than his teacher and his school. Of course, he still felt the sting of disappointment, so we were glad when Frank came home with news that changed the subject.

"Remember when those media vans came to the protests?"

"Sure. I think I'm always scanning for them the way a goat is always scanning for wolves."

"I felt the same, so I did some research."

"Good news, I hope."

"Not really."

I stopped cooking and sat down.

"Our new parent company wants to buy TV advertising for Chi-Z. They asked me to look into it, so I started chatting with people in the broadcasting world. One topic led to another and I was able to learn that Blue Water bought advertising for their medications right before those channels covered the protests. Then Blue Water suddenly stopped advertising and TV coverage of the protests stopped."

"Why did Blue Water stop advertising?"

"They decided that influencer marketing on social media works better. They found people with big followings who were willing to say that the pills changed their lives."

"I wonder what will happen when BrainPill is released."

"I bet they've lined up influencers with sincere stories about miracle results," said Frank. "Let's ask the kids to keep an eye out for it."

After dinner, Matt went out to the goatyard. He didn't come back for a while, and I hate to say I snooped on him, but I guess that's what I did.

I was surprised that he actually welcomed me. "Look at this experiment I set up. When I see a goat shove another goat, I give it a raisin. And you can see that it quickly starts shoving more. I got it all on video!"

He handed me some raisins. In a short time, we created a couple of shoving machines. "Aggression is partly learned and partly natural," he said, speaking like a mature scientist. "This would be a great debate topic!" Matt said. "Resolved:

Rewarding bad behavior creates more bad behavior." Then he ran into the house to edit the video, calling back, "Don't worry, I'll untrain them tomorrow."

I went to tell Buck what we'd been up to. Instead of being annoyed, he said, "You can help me train that little spotted one there. It's too timid. It hasn't learned to defend itself yet."

The next day after school, Matt went right to the goatyard and set up his camera and tripod. He pulled out the goats we trained last night and rewarded them every time they got close to another goat but did not touch it. And it worked! The aggression stopped.

I asked him how things were going with the debate team, and he said he planned to show the video to the debate coach before proposing the new topic. He finished the 5-minute video late that night, and sent a link to everyone, including the whole debate team. The next day, he asked the debate coach to watch it. Then he texted me: "Now I understand cognitive dissonance."

When he got home, he explained that the teacher refused to watch it, saying: "I'm anti-violence, so why should I watch your propaganda."

"I was really upset at first," Matt told me. "Why would she call it propaganda? Then I remembered that people denigrate new information when it conflicts with old beliefs, so it's not really about me."

"Exactly. Remember that her place in the herd is at stake. She rises in the herd's hierarchy if she helps fight the enemy, and she falls if she fails to defend their shared beliefs."

"I see this with kids at school! Every group of friends seems to have an enemy that they talk about all the time. Like the kids who follow one kind of music trash the kids who follow different music. Now I see why there's so much trash talk."

"The amazing thing is that when a group doesn't have an enemy to focus on, they start fighting each other. The social rivalry impulse runs deep! When you know it's a natural impulse, you don't get so caught up in the details."

"But it still makes me mad. The debate coach always says that evidence is important, but she only wants evidence that fits her beliefs."

"Yeah, it makes me mad too. But remember that the world is full of raisins so if you can't get one from her you can find others."

9

Influence

Frank got to thinking about influencer marketing. He saw that it could be good for Chi-Z even though he hated it for BrainPill. He steered our corporate parent toward social media instead of TV advertising, and managed to get Chi-Z into online cooking shows.

Then he went after health and wellness shows, which led him to cross paths with BrainPill. He was scheduled to talk to a wellness guru but she bumped him at the last minute. She said "I have a whale on the hook and have to pay the bills." Frank started monitoring her feed for clues, and in a few days, the word "BrainPill" appeared. It was a teaser for an upcoming episode.

Frank hoped to pump her for details so he made a casual comment: "I feel like I need a brain pill! Where can I get one?" The influencer replied that they'd go on sale next month, but she owed him a favor, she'd give him one of her samples. The next day, Frank opened his palm to show us a pill with the BrainPill logo stamped on it. We were awed.

"I wonder what's in it?" Matt said. "Do you know anyone with a lab that can analyze it?"

"Let's give it to the goats," Andrea said.

That idea tantalized me, but I imagined Buck's reaction.

"Let's give it to a fish," Matt said. "I saw a fish tank in a restaurant recently."

"That's not right," Frank said. "We would have to get our own fish tank. We could set up two to have a control group." He was obviously taking it seriously.

"We could get a third tank and feed them an energy drink!" Andrea said.

"I'll take video so we can analyze their behavior," Matt said.

"Great! Can we go buy the fish now?" Andrea said.

I was surprised that Frank was going along with this. I didn't have a better idea, and citizen science was a good way to channel our energy. We bought three fish tanks and got to work.

Both sets of drugged fish swam faster than the control group, we observed. But it didn't last. Soon, they seemed to collapse in exhaustion. We could only do one trial until we could get more BrainPill.

Until then, Matt ran experiments with the energy drink. He gave the fish of more it every time their energy lagged, and soon, they were so depleted that they just floated at the surface. He was afraid he killed them, but they finally revived. He documented it all on video.

As his powers of observation developed, he noticed that the "energized" fish swam less efficiently. He developed a way to analyze the efficiency of their swim with biophysics research he found on the internet. His video showed how the energy drink wasted their energy in the long run.

The BrainPill launch was still two weeks away, so Matt got the idea of using real ADHD medication in his experiment. I took this as idle chatter since I didn't know how easily he could get it. He asked a friend who asked a friend, and the next day, his piggy bank was lighter but his fist was full of pills.

The fish reacted to the pills as they did to the energy drink, but faster. The inefficiency and the crash were just as accelerated as the initial boost. Matt added the results to his video.

Three days before the BrainPill launch, Matt realized that local shops probably had them in stock already. So he went to the store where he bought the energy drinks and turned on the charm. Sure enough, he came home with a full bottle! He begged me for permission to stay home from school the next day so he could finish the video. I agreed just this once. He got to work, and found that the pills had the same effect as the energy drink, but weaker.

So on BrainPill's launch day, Matt's launched his "Fish Frenzy" video, and we all sent the link to everyone we knew.

Blue Water launched with a huge marketing campaign. It was well-received by students who were already familiar with the concept of "study drugs." Matt's video did not get the reaction he expected. Kids mostly asked him where he got the BrainPills and if he had more. It was as if they only saw the first part where the fish swam faster and missed the part about wasted energy. They heard what they wanted to hear.

Matt was surprised, so he asked why they wanted the pills. They usually mentioned a test that they didn't finish studying for.

Soon, parents were talking about BrainPill too – for themselves as well as their kids. Many parents saw it as the answer to their prayers. They felt disorganized or behind schedule and believed the pill would fix it. When I asked questions, they often hinted at feelings of inadequacy dating back to their school years. Clearly, they had wired in negative expectations about their efficacy, and the pills helped them generate positive expectations. Just like the Scarecrow in Oz. Positive expectations are good, but basing them on skill building is better than basing them on nothing.

The BrainPill buzz continued for weeks and I started to get curious. I had piles of mess in my office that had accumulated in the busy Chi-Z start-up years. I had the time to tackle them but somehow I kept failing to do it. I got upset every time I looked at these mess piles. They seemed to be holding me back from whatever was my next step in life. I started imagining that BrainPill could get me to do it. I was ashamed of this thought, so I brought home a bottle in a brown paper bag and hid it in my desk.

But I couldn't keep a secret. I told Frank about it, and he said he'd clean up the garage if I gave him some. The kids figured out what we were doing and offered to clean out their closets. We agreed to discuss the effects over a pizza after our work was done.

It took a whole weekend to clear our messes, with one pill per day. While waiting for the pizza to be delivered, we decided to make our analysis scientific by writing our opinions down before we shared them out loud. Each of us found no noticeable effect beyond the usual fortification of social accountability and anticipating pizza.

But the bright magenta BrainPill package kept appearing everywhere. Matt said a candidate for class president promised to get BrainPill into the vending machines. Andrea wanted to feed one to the rabbit in her classroom. The teacher said no, but the next week, Andrea saw the magenta packaging in the teacher's waste basket.

Rodolfo was affected by the fad in a different way. "Parents are telling me that their kid has Knowledge Resistance Disorder. They're hearing about it on parenting podcasts and social media. They're expecting me to get their kid treatment for it. I don't know what to tell them."

"Why not tell them the truth?"

"What is the truth?"

"That learning is a neural pathway built by repetition and reward. Anyone can build new pathways with repetition and reward. The real Knowledge Resistance

Disorder is resisting the facts about how knowledge is built."

"But fear is part of the equation," she said. "Once a person fails at a learning task, fear chemicals wire in the expectation of failure."

"You're right, *that* is knowledge resistance disorder. People would benefit from knowing that."

"But if I said that, parents would just want pills for the fear. Those drugs slow the brain and make things worse."

"We know how to fix this. Put the raisin closer. Make the steps small enough for the student to succeed. Once they get the raisin, it wires them to expect more success."

"Unfortunately, parents have negative expectations that have been reinforced for decades. On Parents' Night, we see parents who fear teachers and school. Kids pick up on the fears of their parents."

"Baby animals run when their mother runs. It's natural. It can be rewired, but no one is offering that. Fast, easy answers are offered."

10

Caterwaul Speaks

Caterwaul appeared on the talk show circuit a week after the BrainPill launch. I don't watch these shows, so the news passed me by until Frank and Matt started hearing about it. Then I looked for clips online and there were plenty. Caterwaul seemed like the public face of BrainPill.

I cringed when I heard him babble about his years of hard work in the lab. I sneered at his thanks to his team for the long hours that made the dream come true. I groaned at his promise to keep going until everyone in the world has the brainpower they deserve. He was selling an illusion that diverted people from the real brain power that comes from effective action.

I wished the talk shows reported on authentic brain power instead of Caterwaul's blather. I wished I could spread the facts the way Blue Water was spreading fantasy. I wished I could put an insert into that magenta package!

But I couldn't, so I looked for something I could do. After two cups of tea, I had an idea. I tapped out a text to the kids. "We need to make another goat video, TODAY."

11

Goat Wisdom

The kids rushed home and we started shooting. We got great close-ups of a goat's fear at the top of the see-saw, and then recorded the moment of insight when it stepped forward. We explained that dopamine makes you feel great when you expect a reward. A goat doesn't expect a reward when the raisin is too far away. Threat chemicals make it feel like it's going to die. When we put the raisin closer, the goat can generate the positive expectations that spark dopamine. In sixty seconds, our video showed how to overcome knowledge resistance.

Then we created an obstacle course for the goats. Matt and Andrea designed camera-friendly obstacles that evoked the daily frustrations of human life. Then we trained goats to overcome the obstacles in small steps. Soon, the goats zoomed through the whole course without hesitation. We even trained them to pirouette at the end.

Our video shows that you can learn anything by breaking it into small steps and rewarding yourself for each step. Tiny rewards for tiny steps are best. Yet people tend to do the opposite. They set huge goals and don't take steps. Then they feel bad and give themselves treats to feel better. They train themselves to fail! Anyone can change this habit when they understand their inner mammal.

Matt edited the video and Frank helped him build a channel. We sent it to Rodolfo, and when she smiled, we sent it to everyone we could think of. Everyone. I sent it to Nadia and Aziz at the hospital. Frank sent it to the marketing team of our corporate parent. And Rodolfo sent it to the Superintendent of Schools.

Matt sent it to Sy, without telling us. So we were surprised by a phone call from him a few days later. He said that Blue Water wanted to buy the video for a large chunk of their stock. Our first reaction was paranoid. We assumed they wanted to buy it to kill it. We decided to say that directly and didn't expect things to go further.

But Sy got back to us the next day. "On the contrary," he said. "They really want it to be seen, so they want to add a clause to the contract letting you buy it back in a year if it's not used."

Now we faced a real decision. Matt agreed to sell if the contract explicitly allowed him to make more videos. Frank agreed if he got a role in promoting it. As for me, I was truly interested in disseminating the information, and I knew they could do that better than me. The money they offered would allow me to put on live workshops to teach the skill. I said this to Sy, and he amended the contract to bless this. So we signed.

To our amazement, Blue Water spread the video far and wide. And it got people talking about building their brain management skills. At the same time, BrainPill sales skyrocketed. It's hard to understand this, but it's a fact. I had couldn't complain because people were interested in brain-management skills, and the value of our Blue Water stock was rising.

Rodolfo has a lot to complain about. She was swamped by parent grievances about the pill. They said it gave unfair advantage to families who could afford it. They were pressuring the government to give the pill for free to everyone.

Late one night, Rodolfo rang our doorbell. "I got an angry message from a parents' group and I told them the pill doesn't do anything. They think I'm trying to trick them so they're filing a lawsuit."

Matt overheard her and jumped in. "I'm seeing this at school! Some kids sell the pill outside classrooms before tests and they're getting high prices. I told kids that it doesn't do anything and they got mad at me. They think it's magic because celebrities say that."

We all sat on the deck looking for a way to help Rodolfo. The doorbell rang again and Frank went to get it.

"Your guest's car is blocking my driveway," Suzi said. She looked over Frank's shoulder and saw us on the deck so she barged in. "I'm sure you had a good reason for blocking my driveway," she announced, "so I don't want to seem critical. But maybe you could empathize with me and see how you're choking off my connection to the web of life."

Rodolfo was not accustomed to Suzi's jabberwocky, so she apologized profusely and ran to move her car. We chatted nervously with Suzi while we waited for Rodolfo.

"She seems uptight." Suzi said. "I think she's coming down from meth. We have a fabulous new treatment for that. I have a bottle at home. Should I go get it?"

I told Suzi the real reason for Rodolfo's distress and instantly regretted it. Suzi claimed to have the perfect remedy for emotional shadows and went home to get it.

Rodolfo came back and said "What a jerk! I wasn't blocking her driveway at all. She had posted home-made signs against parking within ten feet of her driveway. I wish I had enough empathy to see what a jerk she is before I ran out to move my car."

Matt picked up the conversation where they had left off. Rodolfo responded with an amazing fact: "I heard that placebos work even when a person is told that it's a placebo."

Frank and I gasped. Mat said, "What a good reminder that we shouldn't take this personally."

"Matt, you just gave me a solution!" Rodolfo said. "This is a universal problem, so a policy should come from the school district rather than me. I'll write that to the Superintendent in the morning." She thanked us for helping her get a good night's sleep.

In the morning, she sent off a memo as parent complaints kept pouring in. A week later, parents were protesting outside the Superintendent's office, with signs that said "Knowledge for Everyone." The next day, each school in the district had a protest, and "Knowledge for Everyone" signs were all over town.

The day after, media vans were all over town. Reporters had no trouble finding angry parents to speak into microphones. We turned on the news that night, and there was Caterwaul's familiar face. "A third of our kids are suffering from Knowledge Resistance Disorder, according to recent studies. No one should be denied effective treatment for this crippling disorder. Our lawmakers must rectify this injustice by requiring all healthcare plans to include treatment for KRD."

When Frank heard this, he started snooping. He learned that Blue Water bought ad space on the networks just before the coverage. We were disgusted by this, but couldn't find a law that was broken.

Protests broke out all over California, including the state Capitol. State legislators decided to "do something." They held hearings to "listen" to these parents. They rounded up "experts" on Knowledge Resistance Disorder, which meant Caterwaul. They issued a recommendation that BrainPill be distributed to all students.

The next week, the governor of California passed an Executive Order requiring all health plans in the state to cover the cost of BrainPill treatment. Other states soon experienced similar protests, hearings, and Executive Orders. Then the Teacher's Union took up the "fight to cure

Knowledge Resistance Disorder." The lure of effortless knowledge seemed irresistible.

12

Neighborly

Suzi's driveway had a fancy new car the next week. A boat sat in her driveway the week after and the car was on the street. She came over to talk to me one day while I was putting out the trash.

"I'll move my car next week, don't worry. A space for the boat is opening up in the marina." I had not been worried about her car parked in front of her own house. She must have projected her urge to control the street onto me. Or just wanted to flaunt her new assets. I did not want to give her a reaction. I wished her well and rushed back to the house without inquiring into the source of her sudden wealth, though I was dying to know.

The next week, Suzi's house was covered with scaffolding and construction workers. She had obviously come into big money. I speculated on that at dinner.

"Maybe she poisoned a rich uncle," Andrea said, having watched a detective show recently.

"Maybe she blackmailed a rich client," Matt said, having watched a different show.

"Maybe she bought Blue Water stock," Frank said, half facetiously. I stared at him and froze. That was a real possibility. I told him how I'd mentioned the groundswell of demand for BrainPill the night she and Rodolfo crossed paths.

"It would take a lot of shares to yield that much," he said.

"Maybe she bought them on margin knowing they would go up."

"Maybe she had help," Frank said.

"Caterwaul!" we both said at the same time.

"I wonder if he has come into money too?"

"Insider trading rules would apply to him, so he'd need a collaborator."

"They know each other. He said that at our very first workshop."

Frank smiled at Matt and said, "Would you like another undercover mission? Do you think you can play the role of a college biology student?"

"In an exam?" he asked, looking worried.

"Not at all. You just go to Professor Caterwaul's office and ask for an internship."

"Tell him you're interested in knowledge resistance."

"Then just look around his office for clues."

Matt accepted the mission, but failed to get past the receptionist. "Professor Caterwaul is not hiring at this time," she said.

"Let's try the truth," I said when he got home. "Write an email to Caterwaul introducing yourself as the creator of a video on how the brain learns. He might go for it."

We helped Matt compose the email, and sure enough, Caterwaul gave him an appointment for the next week. Matt was scared, and I wondered if we were asking too much of a high-school senior. We coached him, but he was still scared. I decided to offer him a big reward. "Let's go see wild goats after the interview."

Frank said, "Sure, I'd love a trip to the Rocky Mountains."

"Not there," Matt said. "Domestic goats are descended from Eurasian ibex. The Rocky Mountain wild goat is a different species"

"So you want us to go to Eurasia?"

"Europe would be fine. And you don't need to go. I'd be happy to go with a friend … if you buy the ticket."

"Yourself? At seventeen?"

"I'll be eighteen soon. You did stuff at my age."

"We'll find a way," I said. "First, let's focus on Caterwaul. What will you say when he asks you why you want to work for his lab?"

"I'll say my sister has ADHD and I want to help her."

"What will you say when he asks how you heard about their work?"

"Mom, why are you making a big deal about this? Do you think he really cares about a drug that doesn't work?"

"Of course he cares about a drug that doesn't work," Frank said. "His career and his power depend on it. If the drug doesn't work, all the more reason for him to stay on top of things."

"Whaaaaaaaaat!!!!" A shrieking sound seemed to come from Suzi's fence. We ran to it and saw Suzi crouched down with a listening device in her hand. She stood up and said belligerently, "So the pill doesn't work, huh?"

There was a moment of silence, which was unusual for her. Then she just flowed into her usual circuits: "You should be ashamed of yourselves for supporting a fake drug! Don't you have any empathy for the lives you are playing with?" She obviously believed that the best defense is a good offense.

As she spoke, each of us spontaneously whipped out our phone to record her. Then we all stared, like goats sizing each other up. Before we thought of a good response, Suzi ran back to her house. We decided to drop it for now.

13

Expanding Circles

The next week, Matt bravely set out for his interview and I sat down to research ibex. I learned that the Swiss Alps had some. I thought we might bring Matt and a friend there, and send them off trekking with a hired guide. I called Frank and he agreed.

Soon, Matt sent a text saying Caterwaul offered him an internship!

When he got home, he seemed more scared than when he left. I was glad to have an Alpine ibex plan to cheer him up.

"He wants me to start on Monday," Matt said, "because he'll be gone the week after."

"I wonder if he's going to the Caribbean," I said.

"No, to Washington DC."

That got my attention. I paused to text Frank with this drip of intel. Soon, Frank was walking in the door. "You won't believe this. When I got your message, I looked up the schedule of Congressional hearings, and sure enough, Caterwaul is testifying."

"I would love to be a fly on the wall," I said.

"Want to be in the audience?" Frank said.

"We'd practically fly over Washington on the way to Switzerland, so why not stop there?"

"We have a lot to do to get ready!"

"What about my internship?" Matt said. I suddenly saw that he truly wanted to do this. We thought it through and decided that Matt should not go to Washington because it would look suspicious if Caterwaul saw him there. Matt was old enough to meet us at the Washington airport for the flight to Switzerland. So he wrote to Caterwaul accepting the internship, but requesting a two-week leave for a pre-planned research trip. "Professors love research trips," I reassured him.

Frank worked on getting into the Congressional hearing, while I worked on travel arrangements. Matt invited his friend Craig and put me on the phone with Craig's parents. They wanted to know more, of course, so I invited them to our goatyard to talk it over. I needed a reason to sit there since I'd avoided it since Suzi's espionage. I shouldn't let myself be intimidated in my own home.

I thought over what to say to Craig's parents, since trekking to alpine ibex is not a typical teen activity. I couldn't say the trip was a bribe for spying on our nemesis. And I shouldn't lecture them on the mammal brain, as much as I love to do that. So I decided to serve them goat cheese and let the conversation flow from there. Soon enough, I was indeed lecturing them on the mammal brain's quest for rewards. Then Frank chimed in about the social rivalry among mammals.

Craig's father Joe said "What do you mean by rewards?" I explained that our ancestors spent most of their lives looking for food and water, and now that those needs are met more easily, our reward-seeking brain dwells on social rewards.

"Our teens certainly show us how much the brain dwells on social rewards" Craig's mother Janet commented. We opened a second bottle of wine.

"I can see how Matt would be interested in this," Joe said.

"I'd be happy for Craig to learn more about it," said Janet. "In fact, I'd like to learn more myself."

I needed to stop lecturing them, so I offered my copy of Breuning's *I, Mammal*. "Teenagers should read it especially," I said. "Strong emotions are easier to manage when we understand where they come from."

Joe and Janet whispered to each other, and then politely said that they'd love to join the trip to Switzerland if it was okay with us. We said we'd be pleased.

The next weekend, Joe called to say that they discussed the trip with friends, family, and colleagues, and everyone wanted to know more. I suggested that they come to the goatyard to talk about it, and Joe said that's just what he hoped for. "We'll bring the wine," he said, and I of course offered cheese.

Then Janet jumped in. "I did some research and found that the goats are hard to see in summer because they go to the peaks of the mountains where it's too high for us to climb. In fall they come down because the food at the peaks runs out, so that's a better time to see them. Could we delay the trip until fall?"

"The boys will be disappointed," I said.

"The goats have their babies at the peaks to protect them from predators. In fall, the babies come down because they're big enough to run from predators." Janet had obviously gotten serious about this.

"Watching the babies is tempting" I said, and thanked her for her research. Joe offered to tell the kids about the delay so they wouldn't blame me.

Matt started his internship and we planned a goat evening for Janet and Joe's people right after our Washington trip. Suzi would get an earful, I thought!

14

Congressional Hearings

We were excited to visit Congress, even though we dreaded hearing Caterwaul pontificate. He didn't disappoint – it was dreadful!

He brought charts and graphs to show how BrainPill would revolutionize the world. He told the assembled lawmakers that an investment in BrainPill would yield enormous returns in human capital. He quantified the presumed return on invested tax dollars to two decimal places. It was extrapolation of conjecture based on assumptions that were pure speculation, but he made it sound like fact.

"But the pill doesn't work," a voice from the audience rang out. I was thinking the same thing, so it was surprising to hear the words come from outside me. Then it came louder: "The pill doesn't do anything!"

Everyone looked around to see who was saying this. The Sergeant-at-Arms roused himself to escort them out, but couldn't find the source of the comment.

Muffled whispers suddenly filled the room. The Committee Chair banged the gavel but the whispering continued. So he called for a break in the proceedings.

After the break, testimony resumed and legislators were duly briefed on the perils of Knowledge Resistance Disorder. Tearful parents and students detailed their agonies and the glorious relief they got from BrainPill.

The Committee was persuaded. They issued a recommendation that the US Department of Health require coverage of BrainPill expenses by all health plans. Let there be pills, said the government, and it was done unto their word.

Frank and I were disheartened and had a long trip home to discuss it. We wished people had real learning tools instead of false hope, and we thought we could make the tools. So we hatched a plan to scale up our goat talks and videos. It wouldn't be easy, since we'd already given away the videos for free on the internet, and pills obviously had more appeal. But we were going to find a way.

When we got home, Matt had a lot to report. "I started drinking coffee," he began. He explained that Caterwaul Lab staff never seemed to do anything but drink coffee. They assigned him to a graduate student, who assigned him to sit with some undergrads and learn what they were doing. But all they ever did was chit chat.

He was bored, so he started asking direct questions. They told him that the research was stalled for all different reasons. "We don't have a budget for fMRI. The molecular work is being done at Blue Water. The Institutional Review Board won't approve research on human subjects." Matt suggested running tests on fish and they said it was animal abuse. I was horrified at the waste of resources, but not really surprised.

Matt continued. "I wanted to say, 'Are we all getting paid to do nothing?' but I was afraid to say it. Then I saw the girl I met at the protest. I asked her to show me what she was working on, and said she was waiting for data to arrive. So I had coffee with her and asked about the data."

"What did she say?" Frank asked, crazed with anticipation.

"The graduate students were running experimental cohorts in local classrooms, where some students got BrainPill and others didn't. I said that was interesting and she made a bad face."

"So…"

"So I asked her why she made the bad face. And she said 'I'm only a sophomore, but I can see the flaws in their research design. So the grad students must see it too. I asked her what the flaws are."

"Yeah? Yeah?"

"She said the teachers are reporting subjective assessments rather than test scores. And the teachers will get significant compensation if they qualify for Round 2 of the study. I asked her what qualifies for Round 2 and she it's not disclosed. And here's the fishiest part. Most of the compensation goes to school nurses, since they have the extra work of distributing the pills. But the nurses know which kids are getting the placebo and which get the treatment. They only get money if they're chosen for Round 2, so they have strong incentive to… to…."

"Influence the subjective assessments in Round 1," I said. "Wow."

"Wow," Frank said.

"Yeah, that's what I said to the girl."

15

Goat Whisperers

I met with Janet to plan the goat evening, and asked her why she was so interested in this. She had a fascinating story to tell. Her mother lives in a senior community and chats with a lot of these residents. These chats revealed that fully half of the grandchildren are medicated in some way. "That stuck in my mind," Janet said. "I think kids need to be given another way to manage their brain."

Joe shared a different motive. "I see how strongly Craig feels about the competition for girls, and I remember those feelings in myself long ago. Young people naturally want the attention of a special someone, and when they fail to get it, they're deeply upset. Your explanation of these feelings can help more than anything I've heard. Kids should know that rejection feel like a survival threat to the mammal brain. They can see that it's not a real survival threat when they understand their threat chemicals."

These comments reinforced my excitement about the new project. Everyone needs to manage their inner mammal, and goat workshops can help everyone do that.

We offered Joe and Janet's group an entertaining demo of a goat obstacle course, and then a serious lecture on mammalian competition for social dominance. Then we opened for discussion.

One person expressed the widely held view that rewards are bad for learning. I explained that this claim comes from a single study that's endlessly repeated. The study reported that children choose to do less art once they're rewarded for doing art. That has been misconstrued as proof that not rewarding children is all it takes for them to do everything necessary to build life skills. This comes from Rousseau's assertion that the joy of learning is enough. We're told that kids will learn all they need if we just leave them alone. When that doesn't work out, educational theorists insist that we haven't left them alone enough. As a result, many children are choosing not to learn. The consequences are terrible for them and the taxpayers funding this.

Frank added, "We need to understand rewards from the mammal brain's perspective. Kids are often rewarded for not studying, so they don't study."

"Anything that meets a need triggers reward chemicals," I explained. "Refusing to study can meet the need for social power. Neurons connect when reward chemicals flow, which wires a brain to repeat any behavior linked to those moments. This happens without conscious intent, so we don't know why we're eager to do one thing and not another. Our verbal brain comes up with justifications that sound good so we never understand the real source of our motivation."

Someone asked what rewards we wanted to give kids. I explained that we're not talking about cookies or money, though they could be used sparingly. Social power is very rewarding to mammals. We must understand this to stop ourselves from inadvertently rewarding undesired behaviors. We can link our attention and privileges to desired behaviors. And we can create positive expectations by giving tiny rewards for tiny steps.

Then someone asked why this is not taught in school. "Teacher Education programs have declared that learning is fun, so it will happen on its own. If it doesn't, they tell you it will happen when a kid 'finds their passion.' Unfortunately, neuroplasticity dips by age eight, so a kid who doesn't learn to manipulate mental representations like letters and numbers by then will have trouble learning it later on. Well-intentioned beliefs can have terrible consequences."

Soon, the BrainPill topic was raised. I explained that it trains you to expect rewards without much effort. This is a giant setback for the human race. Our ancestors had to make huge efforts to survive. They foraged constantly for food and water and firewood, and if they failed, they felt the pain of hunger and thirst and cold. They learned to persevere until their efforts got real-world results. We have inherited a brain designed to persevere in order to get rewards and relieve pain. If a young brain gets rewards without persevering, it doesn't build the skills necessary to meet its needs in the future.

One dad said that he read *Habits of a Happy Brain*, so he understood all this, but how could he get his kids and his employees to understand it?"

I explained mirror neurons. A goat mirrors the goats around it and a human child mirrors the people around it. Mirror neurons zoom in on behaviors that bring rewards or avoid pain, so your kids and coworkers easily notice when you get rewards or pain. Let them see you getting rewarded for the behaviors you want them to learn. They may resist with their verbal brain, but their mirror neurons absorb more than we realize."

"You can also send them to this workshop to learn from the goats!" Frank added. Chatter erupted throughout the yard and I hoped it was about sending people to our workshop. I didn't want to lose the momentum, so I whispered to Frank: "Can you set-up a calendar tonight?" He said yes, so I announced that they could sign up their kids and coworkers at breakfast tomorrow.

Then a question came up about the wild goat trip. People wanted to know if they could join us, and I said that the details would be on our website this weekend. Frank laughed out loud because there was no website. He knew he'd be setting it up fast.

When the meeting ended and the mingling began, I rushed over to Matt to apologize for allowing strangers into his dream trip. We came up with a great compromise: we'd go ourselves a week early, and give Matt a leadership role with any teens who joined in.

When everyone finally left, I checked in with Frank. He was of course surprised by the sudden to-do list, but glad to have a project of our own again. He even envisioned his professional colleagues taking the workshop.

The next morning, he sat down to create the website. "What should we call it? How about 'Trek to the Mammal Brain'?"

I loved it. We designed two separate programs: a goatyard workshop on our inner mammal and a wild-goat trek in Switzerland.

16

Snowballing

Sign-ups were slow at first. Maybe the world wasn't waiting for a goat-brain class.

We asked for feedback from Joe and Janet's people. They told us that their friends and family didn't get it, and they wouldn't listen to a long explanation. Then I remembered Matt's popular goat video. People will listen to an explanation packaged with cute furry animals, so we made another goat video to tell our story.

Then we got a great testimonial by accident. Craig told us "Now I see why girls all seem to want the same guy. And I see why people feel so strongly about social comparisons. It was a great relief for me to know that this is all natural. I can stop feeling like something is wrong." We put this comment on the website because it was a perfect expression of what our method had to offer. Then we asked Craig to say it on video and put that on a special web page aimed at teens. Some teens would prefer pills but some would be glad to find their power.

Joe discussed our workshops with his co-workers and his cycling club, and gently pointed out the social comparisons they often made. Some of them resented this, but others went to our website and were glad to hear the facts..

Rodolfo spread the word among teachers. Some of them saw it as a threat to everything they believed in, but others were glad to have a new tool to deal with classroom chaos.

Doug Kovich spread the word among zookeepers and veterinarians. Some of them preferred the peace-and-love view of nature, but some saw how well this explained their lived experience.

Nadia and Aziz spread the word among healthcare workers. Some of them dismissed our content as "junk science," but others found huge stress relief in the facts about our emotional brain.

One satisfied customer told another, and in three months, we were filling all the seats in our workshops. Andrea was thrilled to be my assistant and Matt was learning to run sessions for teens on his own, and decided to take a gap year instead of going to college in the fall.

At the end of each workshop, I walked with people to the exit, always alert for incursions from Suzi. Frank was not worried about her. "Maybe she'll learn something," he said.

After five months, there was so much demand that we scheduled two workshops a day. We wondered where the demand was coming from, so we started asking people when they enrolled. They often told us that someone they knew took the workshop and suddenly seemed calmer. They also noticed more energy in our graduates, and we knew it was because they stopped wasting energy on the inevitable drama among mammals.

Of course we paused the workshops for our long-awaited trip to the Alps. Fifteen people signed up to join us, of which five were teens. It was a perfect number for sharing the cost of a nice chalet and a safe hiking guide.

Part 3

Two Years Later

1

Crowd Sourcing

The Third Annual Trek for the Mammal Brain was about to begin. We rented the lodge on a beautiful Swiss goat farm to accommodate the delegations arriving from schools, hospitals, and corporations. A big unveiling of our advanced rewiring course was planned.

Before the conference, we had our annual hike to the wild ibex. More people joined each year, which was not great for animal sightings, but great for chatting with people who understood mammalian impulses. Each year, the hike stumbled onto something new. This year, we saw an eagle grab a baby ibex and fly off with it. It was shocking and sad, but it really helped us understand our natural alarm system.

Twenty-year-old Matt led the teen group. At evening campfires, he led discussions on burning topics, like why animals are so picky about who they mate with, and why studying feels bad.

One night, the talk was led by seventeen-year-old Andrea. She told them "When we first moved to the farm, all I cared about was the cuteness of goats. I was really surprised by all the conflict I saw. Then I started watching nature videos. I saw a mother goat hit the baby of her herd mate. I saw female goats shove each other to get food. And of course I saw females choose whichever male won the skull-banging contest. Finally, I realized that lying about biology is not helpful. We can manage our emotions better when we know where they come from." I was so proud.

When the hike ended and we reached the conference site, we received shocking news: Caterwaul was in jail.

He was convicted of falsifying data in submissions to the Food and Drug Administration. I was dying to know how they finally nailed him. Matt had quit long ago, so my information pipeline had dried up.

Media coverage of Caterwaul's arrest was surprising. He was depicted as the hero who cured Knowledge Resistance Disorder and now was unjustly martyred. This view was shared by many of our conference attendees, to my surprise. I wasn't sure if they really believed it or just followed the herd. Either way, Caterwaul's name permeated the air of our Alpine hideaway.

To accommodate this interest, I decided to add a panel on Knowledge Resistance Disorder to our opening session. But I had to go on stage in minutes to give the welcome speech, so I asked Frank to populate the panel. I was confident that our august audience held appropriate talent.

We discussed it in the wings of the stage, waiting for the opening bell. We looked out at the sea of faces and I could swear I saw the unwelcome face of our neighbor Suzi. I thought it must be a hallucination, but when I stared at her, she waved and got up to approach us. I couldn't deal with that stress before giving a talk, so I walked up to the podium and left it to Frank.

He walked down to head her off and they met in a side aisle. I saw her whispering to him while I spoke on the history of our event and the joy of making peace with your inner mammal. Suzi kept talking and they walked away together. I kept talking, but it was hard. When I finished my speech and the audience left for a coffee break, Frank still hadn't returned.

He didn't appear until the coffee break was over and the panel needed to start. Even then, he had a phone glued to his ear. It wasn't even his phone. "Did you recruit a panel?" I fumed.

"Suzi can do it."

"What? You're crazy."

"You won't believe what she has to say." He grasped my arm to walk back to the stage, where Suzi was already standing in the wings. His other hand kept the phone to his ear.

I had to trust him because it was starting time. I had always trusted him, but this was asking a lot. I didn't trust him calmly. I trusted him with huge palpitations.

I called the next session to order and Frank introduced Suzi as Special Assistant to the Director of Addiction Medicine at Sagacity Hospital. She took the podium, and Frank put the phone back to his ear as we took seats in the front row.

2

Suzi Speaks

"I've changed a lot in the past few years," she began. "I didn't want to change and actively fought it. But my brain was exposed to new information over and over until I built a new lens. This story is intertwined with Jules Caterwaul's story. Let me start at the beginning.

"I became an addict at age fifteen. I was in and out of treatment for twelve years before I got clean. In a sense, I never really left treatment because I just switched to the other side of the desk. Now I give treatment to addicts, and one of them was Jules.

"I remained addicted to drama after I stopped taking drugs. I was always surging with anger and pointing fingers of blame. Then, I started learning from goats. I saw how they shove each other when they can get away with it. At first I blamed the farmer for the shoving, but in time, I saw that goats have agency. They fight when they choose to fight. That helped me see my own agency. To be blunt, I saw that I was choosing to start fights."

"It took a long time for me to make a new choice. Old choices comes easily because the brain's electricity flows into the channels that have grown large from use. New choices feel wrong because your electricity doesn't flow there on its own. You have to stop doing other things and push it. That's a complex skill, but anyone can learn it. Each time you make a new choice, you build a new neural pathway that makes it easier the next time."

People applauded. Suzi went on.

"All mammals seek social dominance. The mammal brain rewards you with a good-feeling chemical when you gain the position of strength. The chemical is soon metabolized, so people seek a position of strength again and again. When others do this, it bothers us, but when we do it ourselves, it feels like we're just trying to survive. You think everyone else is trying to dominate and you're just fighting back. But when you understand the brain, you can accept that you are a mammal like everyone else."

More applause. Suzi kept going.

"I'm not saying it's good to be selfish. I'm saying it's good to be honest. When you lie to yourself about your self-interested motives, the world looks like a bad place. Then you give yourself permission to be bad too. But when you see that you're a mammal like everyone else, you know that we're all responsible for managing this difficult brain we've inherited. You can pride yourself on managing your inner mammal instead of just focusing on the flaws of others.

"I could not have figured this out on my own. I was lucky that the mammalian facts of life dripped into my brain over and over until I finally got it."

Frank suddenly stood up and ran out of the auditorium while whispering into his phone. Suzi hesitated and rambled. Then Frank re-entered the auditorium and gave Suzi a big thumbs up from the back of the room. She brightened up quickly.

"And now, I have great news. Jules Caterwaul was one of the many people I met in treatment. Do you want to hear about it from me, or would you like to hear directly from him?"

The room went completely silent.

"Professor Caterwaul has agreed to talk to this group about his mammalian journey, from prison. Authorities have agreed to host a live teleconference from his detention facility during our closing session on Friday."

A gleeful sound gushed from a thousand mouths at once, making a sound that reminded me of a wildebeest migration video.

I did not share their glee. I was furious that Frank would risk everything we'd worked for with this, and without even consulting me. I wanted to go back and rage at him, but Suzi's speech was ending so I needed to take the podium to thank her and announce lunch.

As I walked toward the podium, Suzi said, "In conclusion, I want to quote Wilt Chamberlain: "Everything is habit forming, so make sure that what you do is what you want to be doing."

I stood next to Suzi as she received a big swell of applause. But as soon as the applause slowed down, she kept talking. "Every goat lives with social rivalry. Every one of us lives with social rivalry. It will always be frustrating, so if you manage frustration with drugs, you will always need drugs. If you manage frustration with harmful habits, you will do a lot of harm. So it's great to know that frustration is a circuit in your brain that you can choose not to activate. I hope you learn that sooner than I did."

More applause. I was glad to hear a satisfied audience, and glad that the risky decision to put Suzi on was not a disaster. But I was still mad at Frank for taking that risk without discussing it. He finally appeared and pulled me to a private corner backstage. "I'm sorry. Let me explain. Caterwaul wants to confess. He wants to confess at our event! We pushed through eight layers of bureaucracy to make this happen. It will be headline news!"

I couldn't argue with that. I was still mad because cortisol metabolizes slowly, but Frank added some comforting detail. "I didn't discuss it with you because I never thought they'd say yes. I just gave it a shot when Suzi suggested it, and they kept putting me on hold and patching in new people."

We walked toward the dining room and everyone around us seemed to be on their phone. Everyone wanted to tell someone that they'd be hearing Caterwaul live on Friday. What will he say? I couldn't believe he'd actually confess in the usual sense of the word. I couldn't imagine him saying, "My research was fake and the pills are fake."

We ate quickly because Frank was the luncheon speaker and I had to introduce him.

I told the audience that he'd been planning this talk since last year's conference ended, and he'd reveal the details of our new re-wiring program.

Once he started speaking, my mind was finally free, and it generated a scary thought: if Caterwaul confesses, Blue Water stock will plummet. We owned a good chunk of their stock, and it had cushioned our workshop business for two years. We'd be in trouble if the shares became worthless.

Maybe we should sell.

I pulled out my phone and walked to an exit to call our financial advisor. They put me on hold and assaulted me with jazz music and robotic announcements. I heard applause for Frank, and after all his preparation, I wanted to know what was resonating. So I hung up and ran back inside. I could call back later.

3
Frank Speaks

"You can rewire your brain," Frank began. "You can retrain your inner mammal the way an animal trainer teaches a new behavior.

"Before I tell you how, I want to clear up a misconception from last year's conference.

"Animals are not ethical.

"Last year, I heard people speak of goats as if they're guided by higher ethics. I see why that's tempting, but it's false and it does more harm than good.

"It's harmful to presume that nature is ethical because that makes ethical behavior seem effortless. The truth is that animals are motivated by self-interest. They cooperate when that promotes their self-interest. Cooperation takes work. When you presume that it's natural and effortless, you don't do the work. Then you blame others when the cooperation doesn't happen.

"The romanticized view of animals spreads like a virus. When one person speaks of goats as ethical beings, people around them start to speak that way. People fear being seen as unethical if they question the warm-and-fuzzy mindset. People seek moral superiority because it's a shortcut to social dominance. So we need to reaffirm that the mission of Trek to the Mammal Brain is to follow the facts whether or not they fit a preferred theory.

"You are welcome to your beliefs about ethics, but when you project these beliefs onto animals, you miss the biological facts. Once you accept in the warm-fuzzy view of animals, children, and hunter-gatherers, you ignore all the contrary evidence. The human cortex is curiously good at ignoring information that doesn't fit its neural templates.

"What would happen if you ripped off the warm-fuzzy goggles? It would not make you a bad person. It makes you a person who can see the world as it is. You will make better decisions. You will feel like a burden has been lifted because you stop thinking things have gone wrong. You can enjoy the world as it is when you stop forcing experience into an old template.

"It's hard to change the template in your mind, and that brings us to our topic of how to rewire. Let's start by asking how goats rewire. The truth is that they rarely rewire. They never decide that they need to change.

"They only change when they're hungry. Goats are picky about which foods they eat, but when their preferred foods are not available, they open up to new inputs to relieve the pain of hunger.

"Let's take a closer look at this behavior. Imagine a wild goat climbing steep rocks to find food. Their brain is designed to weigh the expected effort against the expected reward. Sometimes they're wrong. They make a big climb but don't find much food. Now they're hungrier than ever.

How can they relieve the hunger? Should they try riskier climbs and unfamiliar foods?

"If you saw this on a nature video, you might be cheering for the goat to take bigger risks and try new foods. But in real life, goats often die when they choose the wrong food. Eating it feels good, but it's dead the next day. Natural selection would not build a brain that made such bad choices. Natural selection built a brain that predicts risks and rewards based on past experience. Your past experience may not be a perfect predictor, but ignoring past experience often leads to death in the state of nature. This helps us see why our brain hates to deviate from old habits. And it shows us that rewiring does not mean ignoring all of your accumulated wisdom and taking any old risk.

"Wild goats do not see life is a banquet. They would starve if they expected food to be served up without an investment of effort. But many people have been taught that life is a banquet. They expect rewards to come without effort and they end up hungry.

"Rewiring takes a lot of effort so we have to design our rewiring projects carefully to get a reward for our effort.

"Your brain has billions of extra neurons ready for you to build new pathways. But it's like having a pile of cobblestones. It's hard work building a road from a pile of stones. You don't do the work if you can't imagine that his pile of stones could be a road. Our world is full of cobblestone roads that were built by people who lived long ago.

"Our brain evolved to be motivated by hunger, so if you're not hungry, you might have trouble finding your motivation. To understand motivation, let's explore the difference between a wild goat and a domesticated goat.

"A wild goat is constantly threatened by predators. It never knows where its next meal is coming from. And it's constantly challenged by social rivals in the quest to spread its genes.

"Domestic goats are protected from predators and fed on a schedule, but they lose their natural reproductive power in the bargain.

"If you were a wild goat facing predators on an empty stomach, you might wish you lived on a farm. But if you were a farm goat, you might long for the freedom and excitement of the wild.

"It's useful to know that domestic animals rarely survive in the wild. They have not learned the necessary skills.

"You will always be domesticated if you don't learn essential skills. You will always be dependent on whoever fills your feeding trough and protects you from wolves.

"A wild goat's skills are surprisingly rooted in brain management. For example, a wild goat does not panic over small threats because that would waste the energy it needs for real threats. Domestic goats panic over small things because they do not get much practice managing their internal alarm bells.

"Wild goats do not fight each other over small things because they have to save their energy to find food and run from predators. Domestic goats can waste energy on small squabbles because they don't need it for survival action.

"Our culture romanticizes wild animals and hunter-gatherer societies. I don't want to do that. I want you to understand the trade-offs. Being wild would not make you happy all the time. If you blame your unhappiness on civilization, you will not take the action you need to be happy. You are better off knowing the biology and building your skills. You can build new roads to spark reward chemicals and relieve threat chemicals.

The audience applauded.

"To help you on that path, we're thrilled to announce our new Wild Goat Self-Training Program. You will learn to rewire your inner mammal while observing majestic wild goats in their natural habitat.

"My son Matt spent years shooting video of wild goats around the world. But each time he came home, he faced the same pressures as other modern teens. He noticed that he felt better when he remembered the mammalian impulses behind these pressures. I bet you'd rather hear this directly from him."

The audience applauded heartily as Matt walked to the podium. "I used to feel bad when girls ignored me," he said. "I longed to be the guy that all the girls wanted."

The audience leaned forward. It was clear that Matt was speaking from the heart rather than a theory.

"When I studied goats, I saw that life is hard for every critter. It's hard for female goats because their children get eaten alive in front of them. It's hard for male goats who fail to win the attention of female goats. And it's hard for dominant goats because they're constantly challenged by up-and-coming goats.

"We humans think life is hard because our happy chemical spurts don't last. Our brain only releases happy chemicals when we meet a need. If you think you need happy chemicals all the time, you desperately try to repeat behaviors that sparked them in your past.

"When I understood this, I felt a huge sense of relief. I stopped feeling like I was missing out or defective. I made conscious choices about steps toward meeting my needs instead of just doing what's familiar.

Big applause.

I walked to the podium to announce the next session, but they kept applauding my son. It was the proudest moment of my life. I just stood there taking it in. Matt had a big smile. Finally the audience quieted and I announced Rodolfo's afternoon talk. First, there would be a half hour break for personal business.

I needed a break. I headed up to our room for a rest and left Frank and Matt to accept the appreciation they deserved. As I passed through the lobby of the lodge, the manager saw me and pulled me over.

"I want to thank you. I don't know what you did, but we suddenly got a lot of bookings. This place has never been so full. We really needed it so thank you."

I was too tired to over-analyze. I just said "you're welcome" and kept going. In the elevator, I set an alarm so I could end my rest in time to introduce Rodolfo.

4

Rodolfo Speaks

"Can a pill bring us knowledge?" Rodolfo asked the audience.

"It depends. If you study along with the pill, you get knowledge. If you don't study, knowledge doesn't come.

"You may think knowledge is old-fashioned. People say we don't need to know things because it's all on the internet and AI. They say you just need a pill to help suck it in.

"But if you do that, you robotically repeat what others say. Our brain interprets new inputs in the context of existing knowledge. If you don't know much, you rely on the interpretations of others, who may not know much either. We can sound smart without having the realistic insight that leads to good decisions.

"Your quality of life depends on your decisions. The brain makes decisions by gathering details of a new situation and fitting them into familiar frameworks. To save time, it often does this backwards. It looks for details that fit a framework you already know. You don't even know you're doing this. It's like a student who copies and pastes their way through school without ever knowing what it means to gather and interpret information for themselves.

"People copy and paste their way through life because they have more confidence in other people's ideas than their own. This is a chicken and egg problem. The more you rely on what everyone else says, the less confidence you have in your own analysis, which means even more blind trust in the analyses of others.

"We have an expensive education system that values pills more than knowledge. It doesn't make sense in the long run, but in the short run, many individuals decide that going along with the popular mindset works for them.

"The alternative is to think of learning as a skill that anyone can build with practice. The educational establishment does not like this view. They say that learning is fun, and presume children will learn because it's fun. If children don't learn, they blame society. It's taboo to expect a child to do something they do not think is fun. By age eight, a child's peak neuroplasticity has passed. While adults squabble over theory, many children are not learning basics.

"Goats helped me see this problem more clearly. Goats are eager to participate in training sessions because they know they will get rewards. But a goat must perform the targeted behavior to get rewards. The education establishment does not like this. They want to reward children whether or not they perform. They say it's cruel to withhold rewards. If we did this with goats, a goat would not learn and it would not know that it is capable of learning.

"A goat trainer never asks a goat to spin in a circle because a goat has no way to know what a circle is. The trainer simply rewards a goat when it accidentally turns its head in one direction. The goat turns its head again to get more rewards, and soon, it is turning in a circle. Trainers break goal into small steps that the animal can succeed. They only give a small reward for a small step, but neurons connect when a reward is received. That wires the brain to repeat the step easily.

"In our education system, students are promoted whether or not they reach established goals. In the new school year, the student is confronted with tasks that are beyond their skill set. It's like asking a goat to spin in a circle. The do not know how to take that step.

"To complicate matters, threat chemicals are released when you face a step that you don't feel able to take. Threat chemicals are valuable when a goat smells a predator. They tell it to run in the other direction, and they connect neurons that help a goat avoid predator hiding spots in the future. But a goat does not benefit from threat chemicals while it's trying to reach food. In the same way, a student does not benefit from threat chemicals when they're trying to learn. When a failed step triggers threat chemicals, neurons connect and wire the student to see school as a predator. Trying to read feels like a survival threat.

"This is a significant problem. We can't fix it by blaming. We can only fix it by dividing a task into small enough chunks that the student gets to feel success.

"Goats learn from experience, not from abstract concepts. If an experience triggers their reward chemicals, they get wired to repeat it. If an experience triggers threat chemicals, they get wired to avoid it. We humans learn this way more than we realize. You can use this information to guide your learning.

"Discussions about learning trigger strong emotions because a lot depends on it. We can lower the emotional temperature by focusing on skill building outside the school context. Take tennis skills, for example. Professional tennis players spend an enormous time practicing. They do that during their years of neuroplasticity as well as mid-career. When you see the amazing skill of a professional tennis player, you may credit genes because that view is popular in our times. The facts about how much they practice get less attention in today's world, so that seems less important.

"We are raising young people with the idea that skills come easily to some people, while others are unfairly shortchanged. This theory does not benefit anyone.

"Instead, we could tell children that anyone can learn if they practice. You won't practice if you start with lessons that are above your skill set. You have to face challenges you can succeed at in order to build positive expectations about your next step.

"Children do not control their own reward structure. Adults decide which behaviors get which rewards. But we don't always do it consciously. Attention is a huge reward, and we often reward bad behavior by giving it attention. This wires a child for bad behavior, even when we have good intentions. When you understand goats, it's easier to stop yourself from doing this."

While Rodolfo spoke, a noise drifted in from outside. It was just an indistinct murmur, but it kept growing. Rodolfo continued bravely. "You can design a reward structure that will help you learn and help your kids learn."

Suddenly, the main door of the auditorium burst open and a pack of reporters with flashing cameras poured in. Rodolfo kept talking.

"Dysfunctional rewards are hard to stop because they're baked into the system."

One of the journalists said loudly, "That's not Caterwaul." Another said, "I heard he was here. I'm gonna find him." He walked out, and most of them followed.

Rodolfo continued. "A teacher can get fired if they don't conform to the approved reward system. A parent can get accused of abuse. So you go along to protect yourself. You may be crippling children to protect *yourself.*"

The audience stood up and cheered. The journalists outside heard the noise and rushed back in. They were grieved that the talk was over, and crowded around Rodolfo with their cameras. She was glad to talk to them, and ended up repeating much of her talk. I was glad to be there to hear this. When the journalists were all gone, we joined the group for dinner. Excitement was building for Kovich's live animal training demonstration the next day.

After dinner, we walked through the lobby and it was so crowded we could barely pass. Angry faces were everywhere. The manager noticed me and ran over.

"I don't know what you did, but we have more people than we can possibly accommodate. They're demanding rooms, but we're absolutely full. There's nothing we can do. Can you please call them off?"

I told him I didn't know these people and had no control over them. He didn't believe me but I was too tired to argue, so I excused myself and went to bed.

5
Kovich Speaks

In the morning, I went to the window to take in the Alpine view. Instead, I saw a horrifying mob outside. On second glance, it was a tent camp. I rushed out to see what was happening.

People told me they came to hear Caterwaul. Professional journalists had pushed their way into the lodge, so those camped outside were just fans. They heard the lodge was full so they came prepared.

"His talk is not until tonight," I told them, "but you can sit in the auditorium if you want to hear other talks."

This was not a very realistic proposal, so I was lucky that the manager came and offered to hook up amplifiers. People could listen from the lobby instead of cramming into the auditorium. The manager looked exhausted and must have been glad this was our last day. I thanked him for his hospitality and ran off to introduce Kovich.

He had wanted exotic animals in his live demo, but I convinced him that it wasn't practical. We agreed to bring one live goat on stage and use video for the rest. With Matt's help, Kovich made videos of training sessions with zoo animals, farm animals, and pets. The videos would display on every screen in the lobby thanks to the manager's kind support. Now we had to figure out how to get the live goat onstage.

People were sitting on the floor in every aisle of the auditorium, and more were arriving every minute. The fire marshal could have shut us down, but either they didn't know or preferred to hear the talk.

I went backstage and found a side door for the goat to enter. Frank stood there ready to bring it in on cue without the manager seeing.

Kovich began, "How smart are animals? People ask me this a lot.

"We hear a lot of research on the intelligence of animals, but frankly, research only get published if it elevates the image of animals. The rest of the story is ignored or discredited. So I've learned to trust my own observations instead of just relying on research.

"I grew up on a farm," Kovich said. "We managed a large number of animals and their survival depended on us. They died if we made bad decisions, so we didn't have the luxury of false beliefs. We went by results.

"Then I went to college. I was surrounded by professors and students with romantic beliefs about animals. To get my degree, I memorized studies asserting that animals are cooperative and even altruistic.

"For example, hyenas can grab a carcass away from a lion if they stick together, even though they're much smaller than lions. This is why lions hunt in packs whenever possible. You can call this cooperation, but it only lasts while there's a common enemy. Once the shared interest is gone, lions fight other lions and hyenas fight other hyenas. The 'studies' don't tell you that. They dwell on the moments of cooperation and ignore the animal's focus on its self-interest.

"Monkeys are likewise glorified in modern research. Studies represent them as democratic, collectivist, and even feminist. When monkey's behavior does not conform to researchers' ideals, it's ignored or blamed on human incursions. So we're trained to believe that Science proves the benevolence of nature.

"I decided to switch my major from Zoology to Marketing. In graduate school, I saw my peers compete for grant money the way hyenas compete for carcasses. They cooperate to extract resources and then fight viciously for the scraps. I saw my peers submit to faculty advisors the way low-ranking monkeys submit to alpha monkeys. I wanted grant money and prestige titles as much as anyone, but I had trouble doing this. Maybe it's because I went back to the farm on school breaks.

"So I was happy to leave academia for a job doing marketing at the zoo. But I did not escape the world of false illusions about animals. Indeed, I ended up in the awkward position of having to sell the illusion, because that attracts families to the zoo. No one brings their kids to the zoo to learn that animals kill each other when it benefits them.

"Zoo people are like farm people in the sense that they accept the facts about animals in order to keep them alive. But zoo people are also like academics: they embrace the warm-fuzzy view of animals in order to be on the team.

"How do does a person reconcile these conflicting views? I didn't think about it much until Claire Jaynes became my intern two decades ago. She noticed the contradiction and wondered why the human brain is so good at ignoring contradictions. She saw the separation between the verbal brain that's uniquely human and the limbic brain we've inherited from animals. We think our verbal brain is in charge because it does all the talking, but our emotional brain controls the chemicals that trigger action.

"Claire showed me that our talking brain is not as logical as we think. It produces logic when that gets rewards, but when illogical behavior gets rewards, it goes for that. Our unique human cortex uses its vast horsepower to help our inner mammal get what it wants.

"We don't know we're doing this, of course. We just want to feel good, and we come up with clever explanations to justify what feels good. You can see this when others do it, but it's hard to see in yourself.

"Fortunately, a person can redirect their quirky brain toward new ways to feel good. But this doesn't come naturally. It's a skill we must build. I am so glad to have learned this skill with Trek for the Mammal Brain. I think you'll love it too.

"To make these abstractions more concrete, we made a video of animals wiring in new behaviors. Before I turn it on, let's do a thought experiment.

"Imagine that you put your toothbrush in a new place. When you go to brush your teeth at night, you forget and go to the old place. Then you see that your toothbrush isn't there, and remember the new place. The second night, you may head toward the old place again. But each day, you remember sooner and change course. Finally, you head directly to the new place without even thinking of the old place.

"We stick with old places stick even when they have no particular advantage, but with repetition, a new place feels natural.

"You can rewire your brain by feeding it new experiences, but it takes more repetition than you expect. You don't know why you go back to the old place, so your intelligent brain comes up with reasons to justify it. We want to believe those reasons because we want to believe in our own rationality. Our verbal brain thinks it's the showrunner, but it's just the narrator. You can redirect your brain instead of just following the paths you learned by accident long ago.

"You can train your inner mammal like an expert animal trainer!"

That was Frank's cue to bring out the goat. Kovich then trained the goat to find a carrot, which he carved into the shape of a toothbrush. A carrot is a huge reward to a goat because it has much more sugar than a goat's normal diet. Once the goat found and ate a few carrots, Kovich put one in a new place. The audience held its breath as they watched the goat go to the empty spot empty and decide what to do next. The silence was astounding given the number of bodies squashed into the space. When the goat found the new carrot, a roar erupted, and each success triggered a new roar.

Then the lights went out and Matt turned on the video. The audience was mesmerized by close-ups of animals learning new behaviors. Matt and Kovich had done a great job.

We broke for lunch without knowing how all these people could get fed. Fortunately, the manager had graciously prepared sandwiches to sell at a low price to those not registered at the conference. Then we organized discussion groups that included everyone who wanted to participate.

Kovich closed the day with a brilliant activity that he called a Reward-Learning Conga Line. He organized everyone into two long parallel lines, like a giant double helix snaking through the lodge. Each person paired with the stranger in the other line, like kindergarteners with the buddy system. Then Kovich introduced a brief reward-learning exercise to do in pairs. When it was over, everyone took a step to the right and met a new partner for a new reward-learning activity. Then another. It was a lot of fun.

We broke for dinner in a frenzy of anticipation for Caterwaul's after-dinner talk.

Frank was on the phone throughout dinner, hashing out details with Caterwaul's lawyers, prison authorities, government officials, and tech support people. Each mammal was trying to maximize the social power they could gain from association with this high-profile event, but without imposing a constraint that would kill the golden goose.

It was hard to believe this was happening. The engine that kept it in motion was Caterwaul's urge to speak out. We had no idea what he'd say. I expected him to do what mammals do: angle for a way to raise his place in the social hierarchy. It's not easy to do that from prison, so he was playing the cards he had.

As we waited for his start time, I finally had a free moment for my thoughts to wander. They finally flowed back to the subject of Blue Water's share price. I whispered my concern into Frank's exposed ear, but he was too busy to hear me. Then it was show time.

6

Caterwaul Zooms

He began with a nice surprise: "I was permitted to hear your whole conference and I agree with your approach. I do not believe in BrainPill. I was misled … by myself. As much as I'd like to blame others, I see that I took a bad turn a few years ago. I liked being a big shot who got big research grants, so I manipulated my findings and told people what they wanted to hear.

"I'm telling my story in hopes of helping others. Not just people who are tempted to falsify data, but people who accept falsified data because it's what they want to hear. You may want to hear that life comes easily to some people, and a pill can give you what they have. You may be teaching that belief to your children. I want to show you why it's wrong.

"I started with good intentions, like everyone. A few years ago, I overheard a student buying ADHD medication from another student. This happened in the break room of my lab between students who worked for me. The pills were the subject of my own research. So this was all close to home, yet I had not been aware of the misuse of these drugs before. I started eavesdropping more and heard more of these transactions.

"Then Blue Water asked me to research BrainPill. I told myself it could be an improvement over what students were already taking. But things didn't go as I expected. BrainPill did not replace substance use as I thought it would.

"BrainPill was not as effective as expected. I should have quit once I realized that, but I was addicted to the high of being a science celebrity.

"My history of addiction was mentioned by Suzi a few days ago. I'll share more now in case it can help anyone. It's not a trauma story the way you may expect. When I was young, I always got my way when I made a fuss. The good feeling of getting my way wired me to tackle problems by making a fuss. I didn't think that consciously, of course. I didn't think anything. It just happened. When it worked, I was happy. When it didn't work, I looked for another way to make myself happy.

"I learned that a drink or two would calm the volcano. I told myself I deserved a drink because I had a bad day. I was good at making my day sound bad to justify a drink. My first rehab changed this tune slightly. I learned to think I had a bad brain, and I used that to justify my mind-altering substance.

"I went through five rehabs all together. So now I understand that every brain produces frustration. Every toddler gets frustrated when they can't get their shoes on. Everyone has to learn to manage frustration, and if you don't learn when you're young, you have to learn later on.

"You may be wondering how I finally learned. I thank Suzi, and she thanks Claire. Suzi was also struggling to manage addiction and frustration. She was learning new strategies for managing her brain and sharing them with me. I asked her where she learned this, and she would only say that she heard them close to home.

"I know my actions have hurt people, and I deserve my punishment. I hope more people will learn to manage frustration instead of making bad choices and rationalizing them. I hope researchers will make good choices so the public can have confidence in research. For now, I don't think you should trust a lot of the research you're hearing.

"One more thing. This conference has taught me a lot about the natural urge for social dominance. It was very helpful and I wish everyone knew this. We humans do crazy things for social recognition and we can manage that impulse if we know it's there. If we don't, we invent fancy justifications and believe them.

"And one more thing."

My eyes teared up because he sounded like a person having their last say on their way to the gallows. I was thrilled with his comments, and utterly surprised. It's the last thing I expected when I planned this conference.

"Every mammal seeks social dominance in whatever way they can safely get it. Every human wants social recognition and gets frustrated because we have to share the world with eight billion others who want social recognition too. The frustration of not getting the recognition you want is part of life. We can learn healthy ways to manage this frustration instead of using it as an excuse for unhealthy habits."

The audience jumped to their feet and cheered wildly. I saw people wiping tears like me. I hoped Caterwaul could see this and made a note to send him the recording.

7

Back to the Barn

We went to bed happy that night.

But at the New York Stock Exchange, it was still afternoon. Blue Water stock plummeted after Caterwaul spoke. Our nest egg cracked overnight. In the morning, a long voicemail from our financial advisor brought the news.

We ate breakfast in silence.

Frank came back to life faster than I did. He checked his long-neglected inbox and saw that demand for our workshops had exploded. Every slot was full, so he made a few calls to book larger venues. He made it possible for our workshop business to survive without the cushion of our Blue Water stock. So I came back to life too.

The news barely mentioned Caterwaul's talk. This was hard to understand since so many journalists were present. Frank said that corporate media would not run such an incendiary story without the legal department's blessing, and lawyers sometimes stall to see which way the wind is blowing. Or which way the herd is running, to be precise. So coverage grew slowly each day, and in a week, everyone was talking about what came to be called "the Caterwaul statement."

Blue Water stock kept falling, as did other pharma stocks. Investors were asking whether research can be trusted. The media avoided the subject at first because they were so heavily dependent on pharma advertising. But the voices got louder and eventually were heard.

A week after we got home from Switzerland, we resumed our busy workshop schedule. The first day back was hard, and I collapsed on the couch when we got home. The doorbell rang, but I didn't move a muscle. I couldn't imagine anything good being there, so I waited for someone else to get it.

"Claire," Frank shouted from the living room.

"Can't you get it?" I said.

"You will want to see this for yourself."

I dragged myself to the front door and saw the last thing I ever expected. Caterwaul in the flesh. He was with Suzi, which of course was expected. Both of them had big smiles.

We led them into the living room without saying much, since they obviously had something to tell.

Caterwaul got right to the point. "Suzi got me out of jail. She negotiated a deal for public service in exchange for early parole, for which I'm eternally grateful."

"You give me too much credit," Suzi said. "They reached out to me. I just molded the details."

"Who is 'they'?" I asked.

"I'm not exactly sure," Suzi said. "I got the call from Jules' lawyer. He got a call from the District Attorney's office."

"We surmise," Caterwaul interrupted, "that Blue Water was embarrassed and looked for a way to restore public trust. They decided to improve oversight of university labs, and they thought I was the person who would know how to implement that."

"That's fantastic," Frank said. "What will you be doing?"

"Well, that's just it," Caterwaul answered. "When my lawyer gave me the news, I called Suzi, and we got to thinking about a different kind of public service."

"What's that?"

"Teaching young people to manage their brain so they don't see pills as the answer."

Suzi elaborated, "Jules wants to help people find their power over their attention and emotions instead of believing they are powerless."

"Suzi suggested that and I loved the idea, so I asked her to bring it to my lawyer. Blue Water wasn't thrilled, so my lawyer contacted the Congressman who organized the BrainPill hearings two years ago. He loved it, so he called the FDA and the DoJ, and here I am."

"Wow," Frank and I said in unison, and I heard the kids give a big "wow" from the hallway behind us.

"But what about reforming laboratory research?" I asked. "That seems important."

"And that's why we're here. I agreed to do both projects, but I can't do it alone. Reforming research is more in my wheelhouse, so I'm hoping you two will step into the other role. You can teach young people to manage their brains better than anyone I know."

"Of course we'll do it!" I said without a moment's thought.

We all went out to the goat deck and hammered out our dream program over tea and muffins. We designed workshops for students and teachers and parents, and then designed outreach to administrators. We divided up the work and defined our next steps. It was a strange new world because we reported to Caterwaul's probation officer. But it was a dream come true all the same.

Caterwaul was the perfect shepherd for our flock. He had become a sort of Robin-Hood figure, so our message would get a boost by coming from him. So we created an online event and worked together on the message he would deliver.

8

Caterwaul Shepherds

We sat at a long table with Caterwaul in the center and took turns asking him questions.

I went first. **"Thank you for joining us, Professor Caterwaul. In your opinion, how can awareness of the animal brain help us find happiness?"**

"Our brain is designed to seek happiness, but it does that in a quirky way," he began. "It releases a happy chemical, like dopamine, serotonin, oxytocin, or endorphin, when it sees a way to meet a survival need. We've inherited these chemicals from earlier mammals, and we control them with brain structures inherited from earlier mammals – the amygdala, hippocampus, hypothalamus, pituitary, and other structures collectively known as the limbic system.

"Your conscious verbal brain does not link happiness to meeting survival needs. But remember that our ancestors didn't know where their next meal was coming from, so they were happy when they found a tree full of ripe fruit or a pond full of fish. Happy chemicals were released, and paved a pathway between all the neurons active at that moment. This pathway helped them find fruit and fish in the future. Their happy chemicals would turn on in anticipation when they saw something linked to the happy moment, and that motivated them to rush toward it.

"This is why you find yourself rushing toward something linked to a happy moment in your past. You don't know why because we're not conscious of our old neural pathways. We're all motivated to repeat behaviors linked to past happy chemicals without quite knowing why.

"And we're all motivated to run from things that sparked our threat chemicals in the past. Our ancestors survived in a dangerous world because they anticipated threats in time to protect themselves. You have inherited a brain that is always anticipating threats and rushing to protect you. The people around you are always anticipating threats and rushing to protect themselves. This makes life complicated!"

Frank asked, **"Why do our old neural pathways often lead to behaviors that we don't even consciously agree with?"**

"The main roads in your brain were built in youth," Caterwaul said, "because a young brain has more of the road-building material called myelin. We are all challenged to navigate life with a neural network built from the emotional moments of youth. When the electricity in your brain flows into an old pathway, you feel like you're just seeing the facts. But if you had a different set of past experiences, you would see different facts.

"Do not think other people got better wiring from better experiences. All children are vulnerable, so we all get wired to feel vulnerable. Children want protection, and we get wired to seek the kind of protection we got it in youth. If a child gets too much protection, they do not build confidence in their own skills. Childhood wiring can never be perfect, so we all need the skill of rewiring. But the skill of self-acceptance is just as important because we can't rewire everything.

"It's hard to accept that old wiring shapes your responses. It's easier when you understand the animal origins of our responses. The social behavior of animals is especially enlightening because our brain focuses on social needs once physical needs are met. We have strong chemical responses to the social world that suddenly make sense when we know the facts about animals."

Then Matt chimed in. **"Why are animals so competitive?"**

"Natural selection built a brain that rewards you with good feelings when you do things linked to spreading your genes. Animals are not aware of genes, yet they are eager to do things that help spread their genes because the brain makes it feel good. Appearances count a lot in the animal world, so it's easy to see why people have such strong feelings about appearance. Protecting the young counts a lot toward the survival of one's genes, so it's easy to see why humans have such strong feelings about protecting the young. We are not consciously thinking about spreading our genes. We are just trying to feel good with a brain designed to seek 'reproductive success,' as biologists call it."

Andrea asked, **"Why do so many people think something is wrong with them?"**

"Modern culture tells us that 'normal' people get happy chemicals all the time. But happy chemicals are not designed to be on all the time, so everyone ends up feeling like they're missing something. We're taught to blame genes and 'the system,' and we're not taught the basic biology that shows why ups and downs are natural.

"If you believe that other people get happy chemicals effortlessly, you feel broken and left out. If you believe that doctors and politicians should give you happiness, you don't find your power to manage your chemicals in healthy ways. You try to spark them by repeating behaviors that worked in youth. When this has bad consequences, you blame a disorder and "our society.

"You are better off knowing that life is frustrating for everyone. We've inherited a brain that constantly wants happy chemicals but doesn't constantly get them. Frustration triggers cortisol, the threat chemical. If you're not facing a real survival threat, your brain sees small frustrations as survival threats. We are challenged to manage this frustration instead of seeing it as a real threat.

"To understand the frustration that our brain is heir to, imagine a child discovering ice cream. Their dopamine surges because ice cream has more fat and sugar than most foods. But the good feeling ends in a few minutes. How can you get more? Your brain connected all the neurons active during the dopamine surge. So you expect more good feelings from more ice cream, or from more situations like the one that produced the ice cream. When you fall and get hurt, you want ice cream. When your feelings are hurt, you want ice cream. Your dopamine turns on as soon as you see a way to get it. But the dopamine stops soon, and you look for more. This is how our brain works, so we have to learn to manage it.

"Threat chemicals create a special kind of frustration. Imagine a child trying to put their shoes on. Imagine them failing again and again. Their cortisol turns on, and that connects all the neurons at that moment. In the state of nature, this helps you identify threats faster, but for this child, it helps them get frustrated about their shoes faster."

"In the modern world, eliminating shoelaces may seem like the solution. But life is full of tasks that fail at the first time. If we don't learn to manage frustration, we cannot build skills needed in adulthood. Managing frustration is the core survival skill.

"It's helpful to know that managing frustration is a skill you can learn. It's harmful to see your frustration as a disorder that's fixed by 'treatment.' The concept of treatment is passive. It suggests that you are powerless over your own brain and responsibility lies with the person treating you. You blame them if your cortisol keeps surging. You would be better off knowing that managing frustration is a skill that can be learned with practice, like any other skill.

"Step One is to understand the threat chemistry of animals, but the essential Step Two is to recognize the wiring you built from your unique past experience. Your wiring cannot be explained by theoretical generalizations about categories of people. It cannot be explained by medical terminology. What matters is the unique cluster of rewards and threats of your early years. Connect the dots and you will see what triggers you today. Then you will know that you are producing your own responses, and see your power to change responses by building new wiring.

"Here's a simple example. Imagine a child is home alone and hungry. Finally, someone shows up with a pizza. The young brain connects pizza to the meeting of survival needs. Another child with a different experience builds a different association for pizza. This child is invited to a pizza party, but their parent sees pizza as a life-threatening toxin. So their brain associates pizza with social ostracism and death. We don't remember these experiences later on. We think we are just seeing The Truth about pizza. When our old thought loops lead to bad choices, we are taught to blame society and disorders instead of taking charge of them."

Rodolfo said, **"How can we change our thought loops?"**

"You can build new wiring the way animal trainers do: by rewarding yourself for a new choice, again and again. Neurons will connect and the new response will become automatic.

"You may hate the idea of training yourself like an animal, but you will like the results. You can train yourself to feel good when you do things that are good for you. I do not mean eating vegetables and going to the gym. I mean taking steps toward meeting your mammalian needs, because that's nature's source of happy chemicals. One step sparks a good feeling, which helps you take the next step instead of feeling overwhelmed and defeated.

"If this seems hard, it's useful to know why. It's hard to send electricity into neurons that are not already developed. For example, when you struggle to remember a word in a foreign language, that's because you're trying to activate an undeveloped pathway. Words come easily in a language you learned in childhood because those pathways are well developed.

"We can only activate new pathways if we give it our 100% attention. We don't like to do that, alas. We'd rather spend our attention elsewhere. But we always have the choice to invest our attention in a new pathway.

"Each time you activate a neuron, it gets easier to activate the next time. But it takes a lot of repetition to develop a pathway in adulthood. This is un-fun, so people shy away from it. You can make it fun by giving yourself a reward when you activate your new choice. It works if you refrain from rewarding yourself when you don't make the new choice!

"Animals choose to participate in training sessions because they know they will get rewards. Animal trainers create positive expectations by designing training programs that their animals are sure to succeed at. They do this by dividing goals into tiny steps and giving a tiny reward for each step. They repeat this over and over until the sequence is wired in. Then, it's so easy that the animal is motivated to perform it for one small reward."

Suzi asked, **"Isn't it dangerous to rely on rewards?"**

"Our brain is motivated by rewards. This is a fact we have to live with. We define rewards in a very subjective way, with neural pathways built from past rewards. So we tend to over-indulge in rewards we were exposed to in our past. We might deny ourselves many rewards, but overindulge in one or two. This leads to a lot of sanctimonious thinking. An alcoholic might pride themselves on not using drugs, and a shopaholic may pride themselves on not using alcohol.

"Our brain is designed to look for rewards, so making rewards taboo will not solve the problem. We can solve it by filling our lives with a variety of healthy rewards that we use in small chunks. This is hard to do at first because your old pathways make old rewards seem more rewarding, and old pathways make it easy to overindulge instead of stopping after one chunk. You have to build new pathways to make it work.

"You may think it's hard to stop after a small chunk, but you your brain will learn that you can always get another small reward by taking another small step toward your goal. Binging on old rewards is a highway in your brain. You built that highway in a bad moment in your past, when a binge relieved pain. Your brain got wired to expect a binge to relieve pain. The highway is still there, even when binges create more pain.

"You can build an exit ramp and a new highway. The exit ramp is important because you only have a split second to redirect your electricity from the path it would usually flow into. Plan the new step you want to take in that moment and give yourself a healthy reward for doing it. Let's look at some examples.

"Imagine a person who smokes cigarettes and wants to stop. They look for an alternative pleasure to substitute for cigarettes and plan to repeat that alternative until it flows easily. They decide to watch comedy for five minutes every time they would have had a cigarette. They would rather have a cigarette, of course, but change is easier if you give yourself an alternative pleasure. Do not choose an alternative that you find unpleasant. If you hate yoga or kale, do not choose that as your alternative. This may seem obvious, yet we're surrounded by advice-mongers touting such solutions.

"Plan bigger rewards for bigger milestones. Our smoker plans to have a special dessert each time they go a whole day without a cigarette. They plan a special weekend outing each time they go a whole week without a cigarette. They will not have dessert or weekend outings unless they meet these goals, so they will be quite motivated. After a couple of months, their brain will flow toward five minutes of comedy when they feel like they need a break. The smoking pathway will sill be there, but they will be wired to manage the urge for a break in another way.

"This plan can be used to change whatever habit you use when you need a break. If you don't like comedy or dessert, find rewards that work for you.

"Now, here's a different kind of re-wiring plan. Imagine a person who can't tear themselves away from a screen. They have bigger life goals but instead of acting on them, they keep clicking on one more episode or one more game or one more post. How can this person redirect their brain to step toward their goals?

"They do what animal trainers do: design steps that are within reach and rewards that are contingent on those steps. That may sound obvious, but it's the opposite of what they usually do. Typically, their goals are so far away that their brain doesn't really anticipate getting the reward. That's why they keep opting for immediate rewards. To change this, they break their goals into tiny steps and reward action with tiny rewards. They give themselves a few minutes of screen time when they take action on a goal.

This trains their brain to expect their steps to reach rewards and feel good.

"If you're skeptical about this method, watch some animal training videos.

"If you have trouble thinking of small healthy rewards, here are some that have worked for me:

1.   I watch a movie for twenty minutes. Now I'm very eager to meet my goal to see the next twenty minutes of the movie.

2.   I bake a batch of cookies with healthy ingredients. I freeze the whole batch except for one, which I enjoy after that day's step forward. I don't need to eat the whole batch because I know I can get another cookie every day just by stepping forward.

3.   I schedule a trip for the future and reward myself with travel planning each day. If you hate travel planning, this is not the reward for you. But for me, I feel the joy of being there every time I research the trip.

"Breaking your goals into accessible steps may seem hard because we're trained to 'dream big.' Small steps seem weak and boring compared to the high of big dreams. The problem is that big dreams stop sparking dopamine as soon as you realize you're not getting closer. You can train your brain to see your goals getting closer by taking small steps every day."

Then Kovich said, **"It's hard to believe that old pathways have so much power when we barely remember the experiences that created them. Please tell us more about that."**

"Let's use some primal examples. Imagine that a lion is chasing you and you save your life by climbing a tree. You successfully changed a bad feeling to a good feeling. The surge of happy chemicals wires you to look for trees the next time you fear a predator. No conscious thought is involved.

"Imagine you're thirsty and you find an oasis. A happy chemical surge wires you to look for an oasis the next time you're thirsty.

"In today's world, a bad feeling might come from a disappointed social aspiration. Imagine that you somehow achieve the social aspiration and relieve your disappointment. A happy chemical surge wires in the elements of that moment. Now you're wired to relieve disappointment by recreating that moment. Of course you don't think that consciously, but when you feel disappointed, the pathway lights up.

"Each person can find their own pattern if they look. This is not about judging or criticizing your past. You can just thank your brain for doing its job of learning from experience, and then focus on the update you want to make. Here's a simple example.

"Imagine a child growing up with a fearful or depressed parent. The child's mirror neurons absorb the negativity, which wires them to be fearful or depressed. They feel good when they go into their room and code a computer. The complex task fills their mental workspace and diverts attention from negative thoughts. From the animal brain's perspective, coding relieved the threat. This is a healthy response compared to many others, yet your life will be limited if coding is the only mind-management tool you have. It's great to know we can wire in new tools.

"It's easy to build new wiring during our peak myelin years – before age eight and during puberty. After that, it takes a lot of repetition. Anyone can do it if they do the repetitions. You won't do it if you are blaming your responses on others.

"We hear that the brain matures in our twenties, but it doesn't mature like a piece of fruit. It's wired by experience, so if you sit and doing nothing like a piece of fruit, your brain gets wired to sit and do nothing. If you want valuable skills, you have to feed your brain experiences that build those skills.

"Our brain is a spaghetti of neurons shaped by a random collection of experiences. You do not benefit from categorizing and labelling your spaghetti. You benefit from accepting the facts about our neurochemical operating system. Anyone can install updates to the spaghetti they have, but it takes work."

It was time for questions from the audience. Many old friends had come, and I was eager to hear from them. Matt's friend Craig was there with his parents, and his hand went up first. **"Why aren't we learning this in school?"** he said.

"Teachers are trained to blame our emotions on genes and society. Research on genes and the evils of society is well funded, and it's the focus of teacher training. A teacher must accept this mindset in order to get credentialed. Educational administrators who embrace this mindset find it easier to get promoted. Researchers who conform to this mindset get funded and celebrated. The result is a situation where being educated is equated with accepting this mindset.

"Teachers do what gets rewarded, like other mammals, and that raises the question of where this reward structure came from. We could point fingers at particular sources, but the truth is that it's inherently rewarding. Blaming outside forces for your responses feels good. In the short run, it feels good to blame an 'enemy' and join with others who blame that enemy. It puts you in the one-up position. In the long run, this mindset makes you feel like a powerless victim, but immediate rewards catch your eye unless you retrain yourself. You can teach your brain that you are creating your emotions with old pathways. There's nothing shameful in this. It's a triumph of evolution. We humans are not hard-wired at birth like small-brained creatures. Our big brain is born free, so we can wire ourselves for the niche we're born into. It's a feature, not a bug."

I saw Nadia and Aziz in the audience and was eager to hear their question. **"Why does neuroplasticity fall in adulthood?"** I was glad they raised that perplexing issue.

"Birth control did not exist for most of human history, so people started having babies in adolescence. Their brains had to be ready with survival skills already developed. People were too busy feeding their kids to think about changing themselves. So myelin was important until puberty, but not after that.

"To see the value of adolescent myelin, we need to understand the risk of inbreeding. This is easier to see from the animal perspective. If goats or monkeys mated with close relatives, inbreeding would destroy their species in a few generations. Natural selection built a brain that motivates goats and monkeys to leave home before reproducing. They don't understand genetics, but their neurochemistry motivates them to seek new horizons at puberty. For most of human history, people looked for mates outside their immediate group. They had to learn new faces, new places, and new survival skills when they moved. The myelin of puberty made it easier to do what it takes to avoid inbreeding.

"To fully understand why our brain gets wired in youth, we need to know that parents died young in the state of nature. The survival rate of children falls sharply if their parents are gone, so nature is in a hurry to wire up children as fast as possible. But not too fast. If you're born hardwired, you can't adapt to a new environment. Being born unwired has costs and benefits. The benefit is that each newborn brain builds skills appropriate to the niche it actually lives in. The cost is that a child is vulnerable until it builds those skills. Most animals reach maturity at a very young age. A human childhood is far longer than any other mammal. The two decades we have to wire ourselves up is an evolutionary marvel.

"This is bad news for people who think we can fritter away our early years and pick up essential skills later on. Alas, that belief has become quite popular. Even 'experts' support it. But it is sadly misinformed. We can't expect to create perfect wiring, since children are inherently vulnerable and wire in a sense of vulnerability. But we do not help children by pretending that early learning doesn't matter.

"Child-rearing is complicated by the fact that children wire in whatever they're exposed to. I was reminded of that by a recent run-in with a misbehaving dog. My neighbor hugged their dog after it tried to attack me. This fits the popular idea that an aggressive dog needs more love. Unfortunately, the dog sees the hug as a reward, so it learns to expect aggression to be rewarded.

"Human children are often raised with the 'more love' theory. We want to hug an aggressive child and don't realize that it wires them to expect rewards from aggression.

"You can do better when you understand the mammal brain. You can reward a child for small steps that are not aggressive. This can work with your partner and coworkers too. It's hard to stop yourself from rewarding bad behavior, but you can do it if you know why it matters."

Our time was running out, so I asked Caterwaul for any **last tips that can help us put this into practice**.

"We've been told that there's an epidemic of mental health disorders. In truth, there's an epidemic of people being trained to interpret their emotions as disorders. This disease model of mental health is disempowering. It trains you to expect happiness to come from other people fixing things.

"A simple way to get past the disease model is to use a 'grandma test.' We're told to avoid foods that grandma would not recognize as food, so let's avoid labelling our emotions in ways that grandma would not recognize.

"A grandpa strategy will help too. Your grandpa took pride in his auto repair skills, but today we're told that our cars are too complicated so we should leave it to experts. We're also told to leave our brain to experts, but we can pride ourselves on our brain-management skills instead.

"Every monkey learns to manage its brain because it would starve to death if it didn't. Monkeys never feed their children with solid food. A little monkey learns to find its own food by the time mother's milk runs out. It learns by mirroring its elders. Every monkey learns because hunger feels bad and finding food feels good. Hunger is an excellent motivator.

"For most of human history, children understood the scarcity of food and the importance of building skills. They knew you don't have butter unless you tend the cow. You don't have jam unless you pick fruit. Children grew up with real threats and boring routine, but they learned to feel good by tending the cow and making jam.

"Today, children get butter and jam without effort, and often waste it. This does not train them to spark good feelings by meeting their needs.

"I am not saying people were happier in the past. On the contrary, they made themselves miserable by focusing on threats, just like people do today. Before modern medicine, you had no way to know if a cough was the beginning of the end. In past centuries, many cultures believed that illness is caused by the evil eye. You lived in fear of receiving the evil eye or being accused of giving it. Humans have always been mystified by their emotions because our verbal brain is not on speaking terms with our mammal brain.

"We are lucky to live in a time when our brain is increasingly well understood. You can train your mammal brain and your human cortex to work together like a champion horse and rider. A rider must understand their horse to get where they want to go. Yelling at the horse does not work. Reciting poetry to the horse doesn't work. Ignoring it doesn't work either. But if you reward the horse for the steps in the right direction and never reward it for steps in the wrong direction, you will get where you want to go."

Caterwaul's words were widely reported and repeated. People started building their power over their brain. Students started taking responsibility for their own skill-building. Adults started taking responsibility for the rewards they give themselves and others. People learned to feel good by doing things that are good for them.

It may not last because the human brain is not wired at birth. Each generation will have to build healthy wiring by designing a healthy reward structure.

Keep in Touch

If you enjoyed this book, please leave a comment and rating on Amazon and Goodreads.

Keep in touch with the Inner Mammal Institute at InnerMammalInstitute.org. We have plenty of free resources to help you make peace with your inner mammal, including videos, courses, podcasts, coaching, blogs, and a weekly newsletter.

Sign up for our free 5-day Happy Chemical Jumpstart. You'll get one email on each chemical (dopamine, serotonin, oxytocin, endorphin, and cortisol). Opt in with your email in the form at the bottom of each page on the website. (Easy to opt out.)

You have power over your inner mammal! You can spark your happy chemicals in healthy ways. Please help spread the facts!

Books by Loretta G. Breuning, PhD

- **Habits of a Happy Brain**
  Retrain your brain to boost your serotonin, dopamine, oxytocin and endorphin levels

- **The Science of Positivity**
  Stop Negative Thought Patterns By Changing Your Brain Chemistry

- **Status Games**
  Why We Play and How to Stop

- **Tame Your Anxiety**
  Rewiring Your Brain for Happiness

- **I, Mammal**
  How to Make Peace with the Animal Urge for Social Power

- **How I Escaped Political Correctness**
  And You Can Too

- **14 Days to Sustainable Happiness**
  A Workbook for Every Brain

- **Why You're Unhappy: Biology vs Politics**